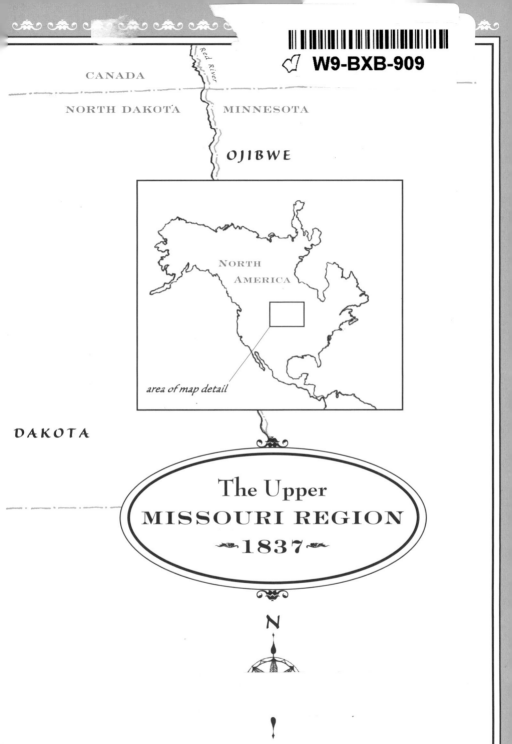

CANADA

Red River

NORTH DAKOTA   MINNESOTA

OJIBWE

NORTH
AMERICA

area of map detail

DAKOTA

The Upper
MISSOURI REGION
1837

N

Last Child

Last Child

MICHAEL SPOONER

HENRY HOLT AND COMPANY

NEW YORK

\

Thanks to redoubtable Reka and formidable Zan; to Jim; to Kylee, a fine, frank, eighth-grade literary critic; and a special *megwitch* to my cousin Jackie, for her careful reading and her e-mail wisdom on many things, including life in the territory between. These friends have made me a better writer; any shortcomings of the work are my own, of course.

I am also much obliged to Frenchie Bedeaux for lending his name, to Joyce and David for the lake effect, and to the many readers of *Daniel's Walk* who thought Rosalie should have a book of her own. Turns out there are some things that Daniel had wrong about her, and some he didn't know.

Last Child is a work of fiction. Names, places, and events are either the product of the author's imagination or are used fictitiously. Any resemblance of its major characters to historical persons is coincidental. See the note on sources at the back of the book.

Henry Holt and Company, LLC
Publishers since 1866
175 Fifth Avenue, New York, New York 10010
www.henryholtchildrensbooks.com

Library of Congress Cataloging-in-Publication Data
Spooner, Michael.
Last child / Michael Spooner.—1st ed.
p.   cm.
Includes bibliographical references.
Summary: Caught between the worlds of her Scottish father and her Mandan mother in what is now North Dakota, Rosalie fights to survive both the 1837 smallpox epidemic and the actions of a vengeful trader.
ISBN-13: 978-0-8050-7739-1
ISBN-10: 0-8050-7739-1
[1. Coming of age—Fiction. 2. Survival—Fiction. 3. Mandan Indians—Fiction. 4. Indians of North America—Fiction. 5. Smallpox—Fiction. 6. North Dakota—History—19th century—Fiction.] I. Title.
PZ7.SS7638Las 2005   [Fic]—dc22   2005009957

First Edition—2005 / Map by Esy Casey
Printed in the United States of America on acid-free paper. ∞

1 3 5 7 9 10 8 6 4 2

177131

FEB 13 2009

Young Adult
FICTION

This book is for Sylvia

In memoriam
SHAWIN-OKWE
Lolita Spooner Taylor
1908–2004

Contents

The effects of the small pox among most of the Indian tribes of the upper Missouri surpass all former scourges, . . . and the country through which it has passed is literally depopulated and converted into one great graveyard.

—JOSHUA PILCHER
(Letter to William Clark,
27 Feb 1838)

PART ONE
Fort Clark

One

What do you mean, you *think* they're sick?" My father's voice cannonballed through the door of his tiny room.

I sat on the ground outside with Little Raven. He snapped at a fly twice, then circled on his three good legs and lay down with a grunt. His breath smelled like fish heads. A wind was coming up from the southeast, and I wondered if it would storm again like it did last night. A blessing for the corn from Old-Woman-Who-Never-Dies.

"Just keep your voice down, McCulloch," answered another man's voice. "All right, I *know* they're sick. It was a deckhand took fever and dry heaves somewhere after Westport. That don't mean nothin'. We didn't know for sure till he come out with the rash, but then it was Council Bluffs, and four other hands was fevered, too, plus an Arikara woman."

"I can't believe what you're saying, lad! A half dozen? And you brought that boat full of sickness to my landing!"

"Don't you talk down to me, bookkeeper. We done for them as good as any doctor—put 'em belowdecks and let 'em sweat it out. The first one feels fine now, and none of the others have died yet. So there's an end on it. I'm not a believer in quarantine, myself."

"Not a believer in . . ." A heavy hand slapped the table. "I've never heard such a string of gold-medal idiocies."

"Don't press it, mister. I'm just here to get this boat up the Missouri, collect some pelts, and get back. If a few red-skins catch the smallpox in the process, that ain't my problem. Sickness thins the herd, I say."

"Damn you for a witless fool!" My father hardly ever swore. This was not going well.

"McCulloch"— the man's voice was threatening—"I've worked rivers and river towns since I was a pup. I been in more knife fights than I can count, and I've killed men for no more reason than calling me a fool like you just done."

"Yes, I imagine you hear that a good bit! And maybe you thought a dainty white uniform would make you a captain instead of an imbecile? Sorry, no, because a captain, *sir*, woulda quarantined the ship. Woulda dropped anchor and waited it out. A proper captain, me laddie, woulda known that our precious fur company can't do business of *any* kind up the Missouri if all our ruddy 'redskins' die of smallpox!"

"McCull—" But the word ended with a loud grunt. Something slammed against the door. Something heavy.

"But, nay, not you! You lay the sick among the cargo—

among the very trade blankets and the foodstuffs. Then you dock at *my* landing with not one but *six* live cases of smallpox! And you let the Indians run in and out the boat like children at a puppet show. Pray tell me, *Captain*— history will want to know—were you stone drunk the whole voyage, or does drooling, gibbering madness run in your family?"

Time for me and Little Raven to go. I stood up as the door opened and a wiry man in a dingy white suit stumbled out. He didn't look much like a captain, or like a dangerous man with a knife. His coat sleeves hung past his wrists. His trousers were cinched high around his middle and hung in rumpled bags around his knees. Three of his front teeth were gray and broken. Except for his coat, he looked like a typical Fort Clark man. But behind a greasy hank of yellow hair, his eyes fairly throbbed with anger.

"Bookkeeper!" he warned. "This ain't over. What Chardon does to you won't be the half of it. I never forget." He straightened his lapels roughly and squared his shoulders.

My father's voice answered pleasantly from within the small room. "I'll be here. And you'll find Mr. Chardon in the Little Village this evening with his 'redskin' wife and son. I hope you'll explain your plan to thin his herd, little captain. If you live to get out of my sight, that is."

Then my father, Angus McCulloch, filled the doorway beside me. In his thick right hand was a pistol. A ring of bright steel dangled from its base, and the walnut stock curved smoothly in his fist. The barrel and the shiny lock plate near his thumb were engraved in fancy cuts and swirls. I had never seen his face so calm. The captain, still brushing his coat, looked up and froze as my father pulled the hammer back with two loud clicks and slowly raised the gun.

I screamed. I scrambled past Little Raven but fell against my father's leg as the gunshot roared. The ball buried itself in the dirt, and we two crashed against the wall and over a bench. When I looked up, the captain was gone.

19 June 1837

Last night a severe storm of wind and rain. Mr. Chardon
sent the hunters out to look for buffalo this morning, for
we had word of a small band across the river. Steamboat
St. Peter's hove into sight about 3 P.M.—the men and
the Mandans all a-frolicking on the riverbank.
Unloaded the merchandises directly into the storehouse,
and afterward raised a glass with Mr. Chardon and the
steamboat's officers, while the Mandan women prepared
a fine dance for tonight.

Later, the idiot captain just happened to mention
that a deckhand had taken the smallpox and had lain
among the blankets and other merchandises meant for
the fort. Now 5 others on board have the heaves and
shakes.

I admit I lost my head.

Two

My father pulled off his spectacles and blew at the lenses. His forearm was scraped from the fall, and crumbs of dirt hung in his beard. I shoved his leg off me and stood up. Little Raven was gone. He was very gun-shy, and he didn't like my father much, either.

"Rosie, lass," said my father, pulling himself up. "You just saved me a peck of trouble." His thick red hair stood out straight on one side.

"Well, you scared me to death!" I thumped him in the chest, but it was like punching a tree. "Have you been drinking? You can't just shoot people!"

"I know, girl. I know." He put his arms around me, but I pushed him off roughly. I righted the bench and sat down with my back to him.

Two men in boots crunched across the small parade ground to us. Other men of the fort were tumbling out of their rooms, some only half dressed, all with guns in their hands.

"*Alors*, McCulloch," said one of them with a laugh. "For killing this man, is no good to shoot the ground." It was Antoine Garreau, Mr. Chardon's interpreter. Garreau was half Arikara and half French, with a deep chest and arms as thick as his thighs. He loved nothing better than eating and fighting.

"That's the plain truth, Garreau," my father replied, wiping the pistol on his shirt. "And it's a fine thing for both him and me that I missed. That young fellow was the new Captain Pratte of the steamboat *St. Peter's*. Wouldn't do at all to shoot him."

"You tried to pot the steamboat captain?" hooted the other man, Bill Swaggerty. "Old Chardon's gonna horsewhip you for sure this time, perfessor."

"If he does, he does," said my father. "The main thing is, I want you to pass the word among the men to stay clear of that boat."

"For why?" asked Garreau. "I been already onto it."

My father bent down to dust his knees. "Well, you stay off it now, and keep the other men off it, too. Don't let the Mandans get their hands on any of that cargo or trade for anything that belonged to the passengers. That boat is full of smallpox."

"Perfesser, they been all over the boat. And you know there ain't no way to keep a Mandan from trading."

My father's voice rose. "This is not a debatable matter, Mr. Swaggerty. You work for this fort, and I'm giving you direct orders to keep the men and the Mandans clear of that boat and its cargo. If Mr. Chardon cares to reverse me, he will do so. But for now, you set a guard at the gang-plank, and double the guard at the storehouse." He looked around. "Mr. Williams!"

"Here," came a voice from one of the doorways.

"Take two men and go through the cargo that's been off-loaded. Find anything that's been soiled by the humors of the sick and burn it. Do you understand me?"

"Ummm. Can't say I do, sir," said Mr. Williams, stepping into the light. He was a short man with stringy hair, and he was dressed in greasy canvas trousers and a buckskin shirt that was stained with food, blood, and dirt. "What's the 'humors of the sick' look like?"

"Right," my father said, more to himself than anyone. "Slipped into my schoolmaster talk, didn't I? Mr. Williams, what I want you to do is very carefully look over each blanket, box, and bag that has been moved from the *St. Peter's* to our storehouse."

"Yessir, that part I got."

"Very good. Now. You're to wear a cloth over your nose and mouth, and I want you to set aside anything—absolutely anything—that looks like a man bled on it, or heaved up on it, or spilled any other sort of bodily fluid on it."

"Like if he wet himself, you mean?"

"Like if he wet himself, yes. If it looks like he wrapped himself in it, or wiped himself with it. If he so much as drooled on it. Anything that looks like it had contact with the bodily humors of a sick man, you put it to one side and burn it. Now am I being more clear?"

"Yessir, that's clear." Williams scuffed the dirt with his toe. "Except why would we do that? We gonna need them blankets and such come winter." Some of the other men were murmuring about this, too. My father took a few deep breaths and began again.

"Gentlemen," he said loudly. He motioned for quiet and then he started speaking in the voice he always used when he was trying to teach me something just out of my grasp. "Gentlemen," he repeated with a little laugh, "some of you call me the professor, and that's a pretty good joke." The men grinned. "But this, right now, is one of those times when all my reading of books might just help the whole crew of us. So pay close attention here.

"Now, the Indians think sickness is caused by an angry spirit, and a lot of our white ideas are no more rational. Even the best English doctors don't know why one man might die of smallpox while the next might just feel puny for a week.

"But, gentlemen, here's something we do know. If you eat spoiled meat tonight, you'll be sick in the morning. Am I right? And, just like the blood in spoiled meat is spoiled, too, the humors of a sick man—his blood, his phlegm, his black and his green bile—those fluids carry the sickness all through his body. So it stands to reason—does it not?—

that if those sickly humors soak his shirt and you wear his shirt, you can take the sickness from his shirt. D'you see? D'you follow me now, Mr. Williams?"

"I reckon so, sir."

"Very good. Now, I'll say again what I want you to do. There's smallpox on that steamboat, and the damn-fool captain laid the sick to sweat and bleed and vomit among the cargo. So I want you to take two men with you, cover your face with a kerchief, and search out which supplies show any sign of being tainted by the humors of the sick. Carry them out of the fort and set fire to them."

"Right. But, begging your pardon, perfesser, if Mr. Chardon was to come upon the fire, I sure couldn't explain it to him, like you just done, sir. About the humors and all?"

Another man spoke up now.

"McCulloch, I know you read books, but I never heard such like this here about getting sick just from somebody bleeding on you."

"*Moi non plus*," put in Garreau with a laugh. "I been covered in blood, and never sick a day in my life. Also, I been already on that boat, but I'm feel very fine. Not sick even one bit."

"That's enough," snapped my father. "This is not for discussion. Williams, you will do as I directed. Swaggerty, you will set the guard. Hawkins, I want you to take three men and round up any crew from that boat who might be ashore. Get them back aboard. If they resist, get them aboard at

gunpoint. Whatever it takes. That's it, men. Step lively."
The men moved off, muttering.

My father turned and almost knocked me over. "Rosalie. Are you still here?"

"Of course I am. You said I could help you count the inventory headed downstream. If you're done lecturing and shooting at people, let's get to work."

"Right," he said absently, looking down at the pistol in his other hand. "What was I thinking?"

I went through the door into his dim room. "What does smallpox look like?" I asked him. "Grandmother says people die from it." I stepped over an upturned stool and moved to the shelves against the wall. Father's ledger book lay beside his Bible, pipe, and whiskey jug. A wide smear of soot climbed the front of the fireplace.

"Rosie, there's nothing worse than smallpox," he answered. "It will make you puke up everything but the soles of your feet. It will rash and blister till the skin comes off your bones. Then it will kill you."

I shuddered. "But the people on the steamboat didn't die."

"I'm not talking about them," he said, setting the stool upright. "Out here, most whites will live through it, but Indians die by the thousands."

"I'm white, too."

"Ah, I wish you were," he sighed. "But you're only half white, Rosie girl, so that's only half the protection you need." I hated it when he said things like this.

"And which half is that?" I demanded. "Right or left? Exactly where am I so different from you?" Angus gathered me in his hairy arms and rocked me like he always did when I was angry at him.

"You are my own true love, lassie," he whispered in my ear. "Never doubt it. You're as brown as your mum, but I know you're my girl because . . . you've got my temper!" He poked my ribs with a knuckle.

I laughed, but I twisted away. "You don't love me," I teased. "You just need my help with your numbers." I pulled the ledger book from its shelf and sat down at the table.

"Wait a minute," he said, suddenly serious. "You'll do no numbers today, my girl. You go straight back to your mothers, and you tell them I said that nobody in our lodge goes on the steamboat, or trades for anything from the boat, or even gets close to anyone from the boat. You hear me?"

"White Crane doesn't want to go to the boat anyway," I said. "Nor Goes to Next Timber, nor Muskrat Woman, nor the rest of them. Only the boys, and who can tell them anything? So there you are," I said with my back to him. "I might as well stay here and help you count the inventory going outbound. Nobody's been sick on those hides, have they?"

"Rosalie . . ." he warned. I opened the book and flipped the pages, ignoring him like my mothers always did.

"Let's see. The *St. Peter's* will set out this afternoon on its way up to Fort Union, but it will leave its two

Mackinaw boats here, and we need to load them with three hundred and twenty packs of buffalo robes and five packs of beaver for the trip back down to St. Louis."

"Rosalie!"

"Angus, you promised me! You promised I could ledger this shipment and make Swaggerty load the Mac boats."

Father's face flushed red. "First, I promised no such thing," he said heatedly. "Second, you will order no man here to do anything. You take far too many liberties with the men. And, third, you will not talk so fresh to me, lass."

"Or what?" I challenged. "If you make me go back, I will march straight to Mr. Chardon and report that you shot the steamboat captain."

We held each other's eyes angrily, and then he turned away with a shrug. "You do what you must. Chardon will find out anyway. I'm not here to argue with a child." He splashed a little whiskey in his cup and stood sipping, staring out the open door. This wasn't working. I tried a different approach.

"Exactly," I said calmly. "Let's not argue. The way I see it, we're in this together. Not only do I need to inventory the outbound freight, but you need me to back up whatever story you decide to tell the mothers. About the incident with the captain."

"Oh, hell . . ."

"Which *this* time will be . . . hmm . . . that you were showing him your brand-new gun and it just . . . went off?"

"All right, girl. You win." He stood with his big hands in

his hair, looking off into space. I smiled generously. I just loved winning.

"In fact, Father, as I recall, it was the captain holding the gun. Wasn't it?"

Father sat down, smiling. "Aye, that it was," he agreed. "I had to tear it from his hand . . . hmm . . . to keep him from shooting himself!"

"That should work," I said. "I mean: Aieeee! Don't tell me there's another crazy white man!" He laughed at my imitation of White Crane Woman.

"He shoved me away . . ." Father continued.

I threw my hands up the way Goes to Next Timber does. "Oh, the whites, they're always doing something crazy." We both were laughing now.

"I caught his hand," he said. "We struggled, and—bang!"

"Aieeee! The gun! And not a scratch on you. Such a fighter you are, my Short-Eyes. Have some stew. You'll die of hunger before any crazy white man kills you."

Father winked at me. "Your mothers are lucky I'm so brave and strong, don't you think?"

"I hear you're far more useful than their last husband," I teased. "Let's go count those packs, shall we?"

Three

⌐∾⌐

I don't like the steamboat," my grandmother, Muskrat Woman, said. "The steamboat is too noisy. That's why the horses get skittish in the lodge, and the dogs howl and bark. You watch them, they'll tell you." She settled into a low willow chair in the shade and spread her knobby fingers on her knees.

I reached out with my hoe to loosen the dirt between the corn rows. "I watch them," I said. I looked over to where Little Raven lay, scruffy in the shade. "I watch you, don't I?" Little Raven thumped his tail in the warm dust. By some defect, his left foreleg stopped at the elbow; it never had a paw. Muskrat Woman used to say it could be a bad omen, that we should kill him and offer him to the Sun, just in case. My father said he was just a worthless cripple—and we should kill him so there wouldn't be more puppies like him. But to me, it looked like he was trying to make a wing instead of a paw—trying to live in two worlds at once. I ignored them both, and Little Raven hopped around on three legs just fine.

One time, my father had taken me and my two sisters, along with Muskrat Woman, my two mothers—White Crane and Goes to Next Timber—and even Little Raven, on board the steamboat *Yellowstone*. I had to carry Little Raven up the wooden plank that stretched like a broad gray tongue from the front of the steamboat to the shore. He jumped overboard and swam ashore, but the rest of us rode the steamboat all the way up to Like-a-Fishhook Bend and back.

Young Wolf had come, too. He had oiled his skin till the ragged *okipa* scars on his chest stood out shiny and proud. His black hair hung past his shoulders, and he fixed it up with mud and bear grease. He painted his brown face red and black. Even I had to admit he was handsome. His eyes, always cheerful, never stopped dancing. And every time the steamboat coughed up a ball of smoke, Young Wolf would jump and howl and run around on deck. We all laughed so hard at him.

Muskrat Woman didn't laugh, though. She sat stoop-shouldered on the deck, watching the bluffs go by. She muttered about her dead family and swore under her breath about the white man's disease that killed them long ago, when she was young.

That was a terrible time for the Mandans. So many in our villages died of the sickness that time. Muskrat Woman and the others who survived had to walk up the river to build a new village here at Mitutanka. She and the other young women built a new wall around the town. Raised new lodges. Planted new gardens, like the one I was hoeing now.

Muskrat Woman was the only grandmother I had left, so I did grieve for her and the family she lost. But what happened was in the past. We have to let the past go, I thought. My father was a white man, so I saw these things differently.

Old Follows Crow and her husband, Red Bull the bow maker, went by on their way to gather horsetail plants along the flood plain across the river. Red Bull crushes the horsetail stalks to rub along his bows and make them smooth. I called to Follows Crow as they walked down the terraced edge of the bluff to where they kept their bull boat. Muskrat Woman wanted news of how the chokecherries were coming. Follows Crow and Red Bull grinned their toothless grins and told her to come along. She just waved them off and settled back in her chair.

"Too old for anything like that," she said. "Too old for anything but sewing. Maybe this winter I'll go to find Spotted Hawk." Spotted Hawk was my grandfather, Muskrat Woman's husband. He died last year.

"Not yet, Grandmother," I teased. "I need winter moccasins." Muskrat Woman smiled, her eyes closed in the warm shade.

It was quiet. It had been quiet all spring; almost no one in the village had been caught or even chased by the Dakotas. Muskrat Woman said this was because the buffalo were so healthy. So many new calves, so many yearling cows. The Dakotas, she said, were not hungry, so they left us alone. But they'd be back, of course.

I loved tending the earth with my hoe. Stepping, reaching out, pulling the soil. The air was warm, and I was thinking of all the Mandan women who have worked their farms like I was doing. All the beans and squash and sunflowers they have harvested. All the Mandan women who have planted and worked the soil like a prayer to Old-Woman-Who-Never-Dies. Stepping, and reaching, and pulling. All of the women like Follows Crow and like Muskrat Woman. Like her grandmother Red Blossom. And her grandmother. All the Mandan women, going back to the first woman who came up through the earth—who came up like a little green plant, built the first earth lodge, and laid out the first farm. All the Mandan women who have brought the earth to life at their feet.

Stepping, reaching, pulling. I was tending the earth with my hoe.

21 June 1837

A fine, clear Ft. Clark day, with a southerly breeze.
Sent 4 men to cut hay. Hunting party of Minnetarees
came in with a good quantity of meat. They saw a
small band of Dakotas but eluded them. Minnetaree
soldier Red Shield returned a stolen horse to the
Yanktonai, and Mr. Chardon rewarded this behavior
with a blanket and a new ribbon for Red Shield's
worthless medal—a trinket he gives to his good Indians.

Old bow maker Red Bull and his wife didn't return
last night from plant picking, which is unusual,
though not if they were younger. Rosalie's crippled dog
also missing since the incident with the captain. And
good riddance.

Mr. Chardon not pleased with me for trying to pot
the steamboat captain. Also overruled me on the matter
of burning the soiled merchandises. The man has never
read a line of medical opinion. Reads little, in fact, but
the fables of Andrew Jackson in the papers sent him
twice a year from Cincinnati. Let the record show that
Mr. Chardon wants to hear nothing of what the smallpox did among the Indians back east. Or down south. Or
even downriver. The Kansa were nearly wiped out
5 years ago.

Four

~

I need to find Little Raven, Mother. He's gone off."

White Crane Woman, my mother, was thinking about something else. "Mmm," she said.

"And I don't want the Dakotas to get him."

"He's a dog," she said. Her hands were busy with a knife and a buffalo haunch, and she didn't turn to look when she spoke. "He's been gone before."

"Not with the Dakotas so close."

White Crane sighed. "He's a dog, Last Child. They don't want him."

"He's a medicine dog."

"He's a cripple."

"He's a medicine dog, Mother, and they'll see that."

White Crane tightened her jaw. Creases sharpened the corners of her mouth and eyes—creases she got from trying to make things perfect all the time. Her face was still round, brown, and beautiful, but lately she didn't laugh much. She and my father were always fighting. Her sister, Goes to Next Timber, was my other mother. Goes to Next

Timber was taller, more slender and cheerful, but she was so impatient. I could never do anything quick enough for her, nor anything well enough for White Crane. And they were always busy with the farms, or with cooking in the lodge.

Goes to Next Timber raised her forearm to rub a lock of graying hair out of her eyes. "A crippled dog is hardly a power animal."

"Little Raven is."

White Crane sighed. "Last Child . . ."

"Mother, you know the Dakotas. They'll want to eat him and put his bones in their sacred bundles."

"They won't eat him."

"They'll cut him in pieces. He can almost fly, you know. He jumps so high."

I was the last child in the family. Not that I cared. I was fine by myself. My two older sisters had each other and their dreams of boys—no time for me. Besides, they were bossy. They didn't matter. There was another sister, but she was taken by the Dakotas when she was a baby. We don't talk about her. Between the older girls and me, both of my mothers had had babies who didn't live. So it seemed like I might be lonely, but I was fine. In fact, none of them mattered. I spent my time with my grandmother, Muskrat Woman. She let me do whatever I wanted.

"Last Child, the dog will be back," said Goes to Next Timber. "I'm so tired of arguments. You just grind your corn."

I crunched my pounding stick into the parched corn. I didn't think I was arguing; I just wanted to explain. This is what makes me so angry—I try to explain something and they act like I'm just being foolish. No one listens. I'm the last child in my family, but I can't wait till I'm not a child anymore.

Grandmother tells me not to argue so much, too. She says it doesn't work anyway. Mothers are too busy with planting and harvesting, drying meat, stocking the cache pits with corn and squash. Grandmothers are for listening and understanding, she says. I raised my pounding stick above the parched corn and dropped it. Raised and dropped.

When he left Mitutanka, Little Raven would have turned north and trotted along the edge of the terrace away from Fort Clark. But no. There were boys hanging about, so Little Raven would have taken the path down the terrace to the river. When he reached the water, which way would he have gone? That was the question. Probably downstream, I thought. He would have followed the bank south and east, away from Mitutanka, looking for shorebirds to chase. But he knows that shore—every boulder, root, otter's den, and duck's nest all the way down to the cottonwoods along the flood plain. He wouldn't be in any trouble there. And beyond that, Little Raven could be anywhere.

"You're spilling everything!"

I flinched. It was true. My bowl had got in the way of my knee, and now it was pitched on its side in a mound of cornmeal.

"Sorry . . ." I dropped my pounding stick and knelt to scoop the spilled meal.

"We don't have corn to waste!" White Crane groaned.

"Sorry, Mother." Now my pounding stick rolled in a short circle on its heavy end and got confused with my ankles. I kicked it away, stupid thing, and Goes to Next Timber caught it—inches short of her own bowl.

"You're hopeless in here!" she shrieked. "Spilling everything. Sand in the cornmeal."

"Sorry. Sorry."

"Just go out. Go to the fort. Spill something of your father's. Go."

I went. The sun was still high in the west, and I felt its heat in my burning cheeks. I snatched up a stone and threw it as hard as I could. I hated grinding corn anyway.

"Hey! Muddy Feathers!" It was Young Wolf. He hopped down from the roof of our lodge and fell into step with me. He went about naked in the heat, except for a loincloth and a rifle he had stolen recently from a Dakota hunter.

"What do you want?" I snapped.

"That's no way to talk to your brother-in-law."

"Go away. You're not in our lodge yet."

"Soon, soon, don't you worry." He fished a small knife out of a pouch and held it up. "Look at this," he said. "I just traded for it. It's Dakota; look at the handle." I took it from him.

"Looks like a child's flint knife with a handle wrapped in rawhide. Who cares? Do you think I'm a child?"

"Want to trade?"

"No. Go away." I tried to give the knife back, but he wouldn't take it.

"Want to trade?"

"No. . . . For what?"

"Not much." Young Wolf winked. "Just a cupful."

Whiskey. I could easily get Father's jug from the shelf in his room at Fort Clark. Angus used to give Young Wolf whiskey when he came to our lodge, but Young Wolf always got so wild when he was drinking that Father had stopped giving him any. He'd be angry if he caught me. Besides, no, I wasn't going to the fort, and I wasn't in the mood for Young Wolf. I dropped his knife on the ground.

"The price of whiskey is up," I said, walking away.

"Hey!" Young Wolf trotted up beside me. "How much?"

On the other hand, I thought, I might be able to pour off a cup and replace it with water so Father wouldn't notice. Or, better yet, half a cup. Even better, maybe I could trick them both: pour off only a quarter-cup of whiskey, which Father would *never* notice, and fill the cup to half with water, which Young Wolf would never notice. I stopped.

"If you want to trade a knife," I said, "it will buy half a cup. But it will have to be a real knife, not a toy with a flint blade." I flicked my eyes toward his belt. Young Wolf had a work knife, a white man's knife with a steel blade and a bone handle, which he kept in an elk-skin sheath strapped firmly to his backside at all times.

"You're joking," he said, clapping his hand over the knife. "I paid for this in furs."

I leaned close and licked my lips. "And I'm paying in whiskey. Let's trade."

"What a beast you are." He laughed, walking away. "Maybe I don't want to marry your sister after all."

Fine, I thought; I don't need a fool for a husband anyway. I mean brother-in-law. Except that if he married one of my sisters we'd all be married to him in a few years—if he didn't get himself killed somehow.

But I didn't care who he married right now. What I needed was to find Little Raven. I followed the path to where it went zigzagging down the slope to the river. Little Raven probably went this way, but there were too many tracks—of people, dogs, and horses—for me to see any clear sign of him.

I noticed the footprints of old Follows Crow and Red Bull, still visible from yesterday. Such sweet old-people tracks they made: short steps, with Follows Crow twisting her right foot inward, and Red Bull shuffling his left heel in that way of his, leaving a shallow drag behind his track. Their marks were as unique as the initials my father writes in his ledger book. I saw where they found their bull boat and dragged it down to the water.

But there was nothing recent that looked like Little Raven. My hunch was that he had traveled downstream, checking on his territory. Past the shallows where we take the children swimming, past the otter slide. I checked the shadows. Still plenty of time till dark, but I really didn't want to be out very long with Dakotas in the area. Sometimes they come right up to the gardens as soon as the sun goes down.

Why do the Dakotas raid us? Why have they always raided us? Muskrat Woman says these are foolish questions. They raid us because that's how it's always been. Our women pray, our men seek their visions and then go out to raid the Dakotas. The Dakotas steal our corn and horses if they can; we steal their horses and guns if we can. They kill our men and steal our children if they can; we do the same to them. Young Wolf went out raiding and brought his mother a new baby when her last one died. Once a year, some Dakotas come to smoke the pipe and trade for a part of our harvest, and we take their trade goods. Then, by the first snow, they're back stealing our horses, and we're back to chasing them across the prairie. It's just how things are.

Along the water's edge, I saw a set of tracks that definitely belonged to Little Raven. It looked like he was chasing a shorebird—his two big hind feet digging deep to launch him through the air, his one good front foot landing two yards later and lifting off again as soon as the rear ones touched down. That's Little Raven. I began to trot now, keeping one eye on his trail and the other on the brush, the trees, the hollows, anything that could hide a Dakota raider.

I still didn't like it. Would it be so bad if we did what Mr. Chardon and my father wanted us to do? Really, why *not* smoke the pipe with the Dakotas, and then all of us trade with the whites together? The Dakotas could lay out some farms down in their territory, away from us, and we could enlarge our farms here if we didn't have to worry about protecting them all the time from the crazy Dakotas. They'd have to learn how to farm, though; Dakotas are miserable at it. Digging roots is all they know, my mothers said, because they don't live in one place long enough to learn anything.

But Muskrat Woman and I could teach them—for a price, of course. And our men could all hunt buffalo together, and we could sell the hides to the American Fur Company. I'd run the trading post where the Dakotas could bring their hides, and I'd trade them for the guns and blankets, knives and copper pans that come on the steamboat. We could get a steamboat of our own and call it *Numak Maxana*—the *Lone Man*. Well, maybe the Dakotas don't have Lone Man. Okay, they could have their own steamboat and call it something in Dakota. Like *Iktomi* or *Coyote*. That's a joke. Iktomi and Coyote would wreck a steamboat on a sandbar and pound each other with the pieces. Those two never know when to stop.

I shouldn't be talking about them this time of year anyway, I thought. They'll show up if I do. Just like the Dakotas.

I'd gone a mile or so when I saw something out of place along the bank up ahead, so I slowed to a walk and kept close to cover. Something large and dark at the water's edge, as if it had washed ashore. How strange. It was a bull boat. It had been slashed and was half full of water. The current must have dragged it until it got hung up here on an old snag. Little Raven had been here, too; I could see his tracks around the boat. In fact, it looked like— Yes, he'd jumped into the boat and had come out carrying something.

I followed his footprints down the bank. He'd been dragging a heavy stick or something. Little Raven loved to chew on the waterlogged gray driftwood he could find along the bank, and he was always carrying off buffalo ribs or leg bones from Fort Clark. Whatever he'd found in the bull boat was too heavy to drag very far. I could see where he had buried it below a cutback, where the sand was soft. I squatted for a better look. His one-handed digging was easy to recognize. I pushed the sand to one side and reached in for his treasure.

It was Red Bull's arm.

25 June 1837

Morning cool, with spits of rain, but cleared off soon.
Back to summer hot, with dry wind and smoke in the
air from the southwest. Party of men from the village
went out to parley with the Yanktonai hunting along
the Heart River. I gave them a number of tobacco twists
to use for presents. Women of the Little Village practiced
their dance, which they'll give when the men return,
assuming the parley goes well. Mr. Chardon hitting the
whiskey hard today. Says it eases his rheumatism, an
affliction I do not envy.

Old bow maker Red Bull and wife were found—or
pieces of them. Gruesome thing, that was. We figure
Dakotas surprised them, dismembered them, and set
them adrift in their own boat.

It's daft, really. You'd think they were English and
Spanish, the way Indians torture each other.

Five

————

I sat beside Little Raven with my knees drawn up and my
fists in my eyes. I should have carried Red Bull's arm back
to his daughters, but instead I had dropped it and screamed
and run home. I had panicked. I was exhausted with shame.

Ten men went out to find his body and the body of
Follows Crow. The clan members made a platform among
the dead ones behind the town and they laid Follows Crow
and Red Bull gently on it. At least it's nice to think they'll
be together in the other world, making arrows, picking
berries. The relatives covered them with a fine doeskin, and
then, out of respect, their oldest daughter cut off her hair
and one finger.

With my knuckles pressed into my eyes, I could see red
clouds against a warm darkness, and if I sat very still,
shooting stars would cross the darkness from time to time.
Little Raven sighed noisily and rolled onto his side, dropping his heavy head against my ankle. Of course, he was
home when I got here. After his digging, he'd gone up the
bank and had come back over the prairie.

My father has a book called *Sir Walter Scott's Poetical Works*, and in it there is a girl with swan-white skin and raven hair. She is very sad sometimes, because her father locks her in a tower, which is a kind of earth lodge on a high hill. I didn't think I'd be as sad as she was about the tower. At least she didn't have to sit on a watching platform, to chase crows and boys away from the corn.

I'd never seen a white girl—not swan-white—only the few mixed-blood girls of Mitutanka like me. A swan is a ferocious bird that spends all summer on the cold lakes in the north. Would a white girl be fierce like that? Would she cut off her hair and a finger if her mother was murdered? Surely she would.

Little Raven lifted his head, and then I heard steps coming toward us. Someone sat down beside me, humming. Young Wolf. On the other side of him, his friend Medicine Bird picked up a stick and began to draw pictures in the dust. I kept my fists in my eyes, watching the warm clouds and shooting stars. I hated Young Wolf's constant noisemaking.

He was a good singer, with a fine high voice that seemed to come out the top of his head. He sang with the drum at dances, and that was nice. But he sang at other times, too—like all the time—humming nonsense words to himself, bobbing his head to the rhythm of his own songs. Lately, he'd been trying to learn songs from the white men in Fort Clark. Unfortunately, both his English and his French were terrible, so what he learned was a few words here and there, threads and snatches, never a whole song. This didn't trouble Young Wolf. He just worked those phrases into his own music, filled out with syllables of nonsense.

"Hey, hey, eyah," he murmured in a high voice. "So they say that the women are worse than the men, owah."

"I'm thinking here, Young Wolf. Can't you sing somewhere else?"

It was like he didn't even hear me. "Hey," he said to Medicine Bird, "hey, the women are worse than the men. I wonder what that means."

"Something about farms?" offered Medicine Bird.

"It means the women are harder to live with," I told them from behind my knuckles. "And the next words are 'they've been down to hell but they come back again.' You don't have to make things up."

"'Been down to . . .'?"

"Hell. Been down to hell."

"That's back in America, I guess," Young Wolf said.

"Hell is where the devil lives, of course. The devil is the white god of bad things."

"I see," said Medicine Bird. "So 'down to hell' is like 'down to his village on Heart River.'"

I lifted my head. "No, you don't understand. 'Hell' is in the spirit world. It's a town that's always on fire. The devil lives there, and white people have to go there if they do something bad in their life." Young Wolf nodded, but he wasn't following this. I tried again.

"Look, it's a joking song. The devil is a very bad spirit.

He takes the white woman, but *she's* so bad that even in hell they don't want her."

Medicine Bird wrinkled his forehead. "And this is funny. . . ."

"It's very funny!" Young Wolf said with a laugh. "You just don't understand white humor."

"Oh, you're so much smarter than I am," said Medicine Bird, tossing his stick away.

"Just one thing," Young Wolf said to me. "Does he give the man a horse?"

"For what?"

"You can't take a man's wife without giving him a horse."

"Well, this is a white man's song," Medicine Bird pointed out.

Young Wolf sighed. "True. Whites aren't so good on giving gifts."

"No, it's a joke! They try to give *each other* the woman," I wailed. "Look, a farmer was plowing his field one day. Plowing is like hoeing. The devil comes by and says, 'Oh, your wife is too hard on you,' and he takes the wife. But when he gets her home, she just about kills him, so the devil brings her back to her husband. See? She's so hard to live with, the man doesn't want her, and the devil doesn't either."

Young Wolf laughed. "Good joke. If she can make a man do farming, she's really in charge."

"If she's just mean, then he shouldn't have married her," Medicine Bird put in.

I gave up. "Well, that's how it is," I said. "I guess that's why Mandan men are so happy. We don't let them in the fields at all, for fear they'd make a mess."

I went back to pressing my eyes, and Young Wolf went back to humming. I concentrated on other sounds for a while. A sparrow called. Young Wolf's horse stamped. I counted the grasshoppers clattering by toward the cornfields.

"I like these white-men songs," Young Wolf declared suddenly. "I like those white men at the fort. You like them?"

"I *am* one of those white people at the fort," I snapped.

"Come on," snorted Medicine Bird. "You're a Mitutanka girl."

"Your father's a white," Young Wolf added. "That doesn't mean you are."

I raised my head, suddenly furious. "My father is white, and so am I, you ignorant, scrawny, louse-eaten prairie chickens!" I scrambled up. "I read their talking papers, I count with their numbers, I speak two of the white languages. And someday I'm going to get away from here and run my own trading post for the American Fur Company."

Young Wolf only laughed. "Whites don't let women run a trading post," he said. "And I speak to my horses, but that doesn't make me a horse."

"It might," I said through clenched teeth. "When you're drunk, no one can tell you from your horse's rear end."

"Ouch," he said, wincing. "Maybe you *are* white, little girl. That's what your sisters say." But I wasn't finished.

"At least I'm not a drunk. That's why the white men give you whiskey—they laugh at you, and so does everyone in Mitutanka."

Medicine Bird looked away, saying nothing, as Young Wolf jumped to his feet. "I'll tell you one thing," Young Wolf said, throwing out his chest. "If I was such a fool, the steamboat captain wouldn't have told me who killed Red Bull and Follows Crow."

"What?" I was stunned.

"Young Wolf, I don't like this too much," said Medicine Bird. Young Wolf shook him off.

"That's right," he went on. "He came by last evening while we were tending my fish trap. I told him Red Bull was from my father's clan and we'd be avenging him one day. He said he knows where they are—up the Knife River, west of the big Minnetaree town."

"How could he know this?" I asked. "And what's he doing around here, anyway? The steamboat left five days ago."

"He let them go on ahead so he could do some hunting. That's when he saw the Dakota raiders. If I meet him later, he'll take me right to their camp."

"You wouldn't go after them alone," I said. I turned to Medicine Bird. "You can't let him go."

Medicine Bird was quiet.

"Just to scout," Young Wolf answered. "And I wouldn't be alone. I'd be with him, too—a white captain is pretty strong medicine. He says there are only six Dakotas. Looks like they broke off from a larger hunting party."

"But I don't think you can trust him. My father says that man has brought the smallpox here on the steamboat. Some people might get sick because of him."

Young Wolf shrugged. "What you and your white father think doesn't matter. You just worry about your trading post and setting your towns on fire."

I groaned. Young Wolf turned away with Medicine Bird. "What's that thing he said for the white way to restore the balance? A knife for a knife?"

"It's an eye for an eye!" I shouted. "Your English is terrible!"

28 June 1837

Afternoon very smokey, light breeze from the southwest.
Mandans are saying the Dakotas set fire to the
prairies—easier to steal horses with smoke in the air.
Chardon sent Garreau and 8 men to find a band of
buffalo reported 20 miles off.

Parley party who went out to the Yanktonai camp
returned. No luck in that quarter. Yanktonai relieved
them of tobacco and weapons, plus two good horses,
and broke all the fingers on one boy's hand for him.
Mandans left, but slipped back, stole one horse, one
scalp, and set fire to the short grass to cover their escape.
Well organized, at least.

Six

Muskrat Woman didn't sleep much at night; she caught short naps during the day. Her bones didn't like to lie still for long, even in her comfortable sleeping berth on the robes and furs. So I wasn't surprised when I woke suddenly in the dark lodge and saw her standing by the fire pit, where two logs smoldered. She glanced over and motioned me to listen. Little Raven's ears were up; he, too, had noticed something unusual. And then I heard the noise again that had wakened me.

"Eyah . . . eyah, and she went to Heart River but come back again." Young Wolf's voice floated gently down the smoke hole, barely audible above the soft footsteps of his horse. I'm sure he thought he was quiet as an owl, but he couldn't help murmuring to himself. Muskrat Woman opened her mouth to laugh silently. She shook her head.

"I don't know where he's going, but I hope it isn't to steal horses," she said, smiling. "Drinking whiskey doesn't work out with stealing horses like it does with singing songs." She pushed a small blackened log to one side with her foot.

A plume of ash went up toward the smoke hole, and Muskrat Woman turned her back to it. "My Spotted Hawk used to talk to himself. I told him a hundred times, 'You better keep your thoughts inside your mouth,' but he never could. One time he went to steal horses from the Yanktonai and lost part of his ear because he couldn't keep from muttering." Her eyes squinted tightly as she laughed again.

"Young Wolf isn't going to steal horses," I told her. "He's off to scout the Dakota camp."

"Alone?"

"With the steamboat captain."

"Who?"

"The captain of the steamboat that was just here."

Muskrat Woman's eyebrows went up. "He's going to scout a Dakota camp with a white man—one he doesn't even know?"

"That's what he says," I answered. She shook her head and stepped around the fire pit toward the door, stretching a little as she went. I got up to follow her outside. We walked around the lodge together and watched the dark figures of Young Wolf and his horse quietly.

"You ever notice how white men get a lot of headaches?" Muskrat Woman asked me.

"Sure," I said.

"Ever notice how we get a lot of white men?" She snorted softly at her own joke.

"I'm white, Grandmother."

"Oh? How can you tell?"

"Of course I am. Like my father. Everyone knows that."

Muskrat Woman shrugged. "Why not red, like your mother?" she asked. I hadn't thought about it that way. It seemed like everyone's mother was Mandan, so my father's being different was what mattered.

"Well," I said, looking at the dirt. "It's what I want to be. And even the mothers think I'm more like him."

"Usually," Muskrat Woman said, "it's more than the seed you start with. A plant needs light and rain and someone to chase off the birds. We'll have to see how you turn out." She pinched me lightly on the arm. I loved it when she did that.

As we crossed the open dancing ground, a shooting star drew its streak of white across the sky. I craned my head back and turned slowly around and around under the blackness. The stars wheeled above as if I were the pin to which they all were tethered. My starry horses pacing through the sky.

We came to Lone Man's tall cedar post in the center of the village, and we stopped. Sometimes, Muskrat Woman came out here just to stand and think. I looked at Lone Man's cedar post in its ring of shorter posts and remembered the story of why we put it there.

There was heavy rain for days and days. The river left its banks and flooded the corn, and it even began to climb the bluffs where the lodges were. So Lone Man took cotton-

wood timbers and he built a heavy wall around the town, just like the wall we have around Mitutanka now.

When the water saw that it couldn't get over Lone Man's wall, the rain stopped, and the sun came out, and the river sank back to its bed, and the corn began to grow. All things went back to the way they were. But on the wall around the town, the water had left a mark.

Lone Man set a cedar post in the center of the dancing ground. He said that when we have our ceremonies we are to call to him, and he will hear us. Around his cedar post Lone Man made a wall of slender cottonwood saplings, to stand for the wall that always protects us. Finally, around this wall, almost to the top, he tied a long strip of willow bark to show where the water had left its highest mark. Whatever may attack the Mandan people, it will never completely overcome us.

A half-moon hung over the horizon, and a breeze came down the river, cool and sweet with rain from the northwest. The night was quiet. In silence, Muskrat Woman and I watched Young Wolf slip into the dark beyond the sheltering wall of Mitutanka.

PART TWO

The Prairie

1 July 1837

The women gave us a dance last evening, my wives
watching me like a hawk for misbehavior. Chardon got
a whipping from his wife, I hear. Besides looking more
than once at the younger women, he also emptied half
a whiskey keg into some of the young men.

    Mandans are set to go out after buffalo, a herd of
500 having been sighted. Myself, I wouldn't chase the
beasties after a night like that. Those old bulls
never have a whiskey headache.

One

~

There were other girls who were mixed-blood like me. Some of them even had light eyes from their white fathers or grandfathers. Some had streaks of white in their hair—like Sahkoka, who showed off so much for George Catlin, the white painter. I didn't have those. So why did my sisters think of me as more of a white girl than they were? Just because I liked the white world as well as the Mandan?

I looked at my hand. The skin was brown but lighter than White Crane Woman's; the fingers tapered like hers but were broad across the knuckles like my father's. My cheekbones were strong like hers but not as wide, and I had his brown freckles across my nose. My hair was dark and heavy like hers but wavy like his.

The trouble was that Angus didn't let go of his life among the whites, like the earlier white men who came to marry earth-lodge women. Like Old Frenchie Bedeaux—he's been here so long he can't stand real white men. My father wanted both. He stayed here, but he stayed very much a white man, with his iron tools, his woven cloth, his paper and ink, his traps and guns. And I thought of those things as mine, too. Those were my white things, just like the new hoe that Muskrat Woman had made from the shoulder blade of a buffalo calf was one of my Mandan things.

I had the Mandan way with plants and animals, but I had my father's head for numbers. I couldn't help it. I could read and write the talking papers, which even most of the white men in Fort Clark couldn't do. Angus taught me songs from his family, like "The Devil and the Farmer" and the one about the gray mare. He gave me lengths of trade cloth to sew with Muskrat Woman, and a white handkerchief, which I carried with me all the time, and he taught me how to use it.

My sisters didn't care about that kind of thing. They blew their noses on the ground. They said I used a handkerchief because I was saving my snot for something. Father gave them a copper pan for cooking, and they cut it up to make cones for their jingle dresses. A metal pan makes food taste bad, but, still, it shows what they cared about: dancing and finding the right man to marry. They wanted a good hunter like Young Wolf, a brave man to steal horses from the Dakotas. That was fine; I liked Young Wolf. He was funny, but not very smart. Like most of the young men, when he wasn't hunting he was on his mothers' roof, gambling or dreaming.

Young Wolf wasn't his name exactly. But that's another difference. With my Mandan family, names were not like they were for my white father. White people name their babies before they're even born. Mandans usually wait till they know the baby isn't going away. And another thing: every Mandan has some relatives whose job it is to tease them. White people don't have joking relatives. They don't have many relatives at all.

My clan's winter lodges used to be near a wolf den, and one year there was a wolf puppy who would sit by the den moaning and murmuring quietly, like he was trying out the words to a new howl. That's what Young Wolf did—always humming and murmuring. So his joking relatives started calling him "Sings Like the Wolf Pup at the Winter Lodge." That seemed simple enough, but of course it was too long for my father. He had to say "Wolf Boy" or "Young Wolf." That works better in English, because in English you have only one name, it's short, and everyone knows what it is.

My sisters wanted to marry him, and I figured I would, too. Or maybe not. But I didn't want to marry a white man, either, because he might go back to America. In America, the men had only one wife each, which sounded completely crazy. One wife to do all the work?

What I wanted was my own trading post. Father said there was more wealth to be made in *trading* corn and buffalo robes than in *growing* corn and *hunting* buffalo. That's what I wanted to do. So my sisters and mothers could keep the farm and the lodge, Young Wolf could do the hunting, I could run the trading post, and Angus could be my second-in-command, like he is for Mr. Chardon. That would keep all the best things from both sides of my family.

3 July 1837

Smoke clearing somewhat, and a promise of rain with wind in the west. One of the scouts came in with bad news. Old Bedeaux capsized his skin boat in a gale upriver. Loaded with 600 robes, all of which are lost along with the old man himself. Tomorrow, Chardon will send two men up to look for a body and to fish out the robes if possible.

Two

My father looked up as I stepped over the threshold. "There you are," he said. He was on one knee, tying down the flaps on a pair of saddlebags that he'd thrown over the bench. Two bedrolls lay nearby, and on the table were his rifle, his pouch, assorted knives, and his new pistol. "Run back and grab some cornballs and pemmican and dried meat and whatever food isn't tied down, will you? I need you to come with me."

"Where are we going?" I asked cautiously. The idea of getting away was exciting, but some of my father's big ideas didn't turn out so well. My mothers had made this clear any number of times.

"We're going to run upriver thirty or forty miles and try to find Old Bedeaux."

"Why? What's happened to him?"

"All we know is he capsized with a load of robes. We don't know if he managed to get out alive, or if he's floated facedown to Fort Pierre by now. But we need to get out there quick-like, so shake a leg and bring that grub."

"Why am I going with you instead of one of the men?"

"Because I said so," he groaned. "Why is it like talking to a church inquisitor with you, lass?" Then his voice softened. "All right, here's the plan. Swaggerty is coming to help me with the heavy work. I also need someone to press the water out of the hides, but most of all I need a clerk. It's a big load of robes—could be six hundred—and I want an inventory of what we drag out of the river. There aren't but two men can count beyond one-and-twenty, and Mr. Chardon has both of them out after buffalo. You'll be my clerk."

This was good news. I would be more than camp cook and beast of burden—what the white men called a squaw. "Still," I said, "that's only three of us, and there are Dakota raiders out there somewhere."

"I know, I know. Your mothers have been through this already," he said, a little testily. "But, look, a bigger party will just attract the Dakotas anyway. Plus, the Dakotas are east and south of us, and we're going north and west. And, last but not least, I need to take care of this problem myself—there may be a bit of a bonus in it."

It didn't really matter; I was quite glad for an excuse to get away. Sometimes Angus drove me crazy with his big ideas, but right now everyone in the lodge was so hard to get along with. Anything was better than staying in the village. "Okay. Do I get to ride behind you?"

"Nope," he said with a grin. "I just swapped Garreau for the use of his little gray mare. You'll ride in style this time, milady."

"Even better! I like that mare," I said. Then something else struck me. "By the way, who's going to clean up the wet robes afterward? They'll be in bad shape."

"Haven't thought that far. Why?"

"I can get our clan women to do it for you," I suggested. "I'll organize the whole thing, if I can have two out of every ten robes they fix up."

His red eyebrows went up. "Why not wish for a gold watch and chain while you're at it?"

"Well, let's see," I said innocently, thinking aloud. "Who else can get it done? The men out hunting can't do it. You can't do it. Mr. Chardon can't do it. You might get some Minnetaree women, but that will delay you. And if you don't start soon, you'll lose a lot more than two robes in ten."

"Yes, love," my father argued, "but you're forgetting that I can talk to the clan women as well as you can."

I crossed my arms. "Oh dear, I just remembered: the mothers need me in the gardens. There's no way they'll let me go upriver this week."

He grabbed his hair in both hands and shouted, "All right, all right! You organize the clan women. But," he added quickly, raising a finger, "your cut is one robe in twenty, and that's final."

"One in ten," I countered.

"Done." My father grinned. "A pleasure doing business with you. Though what you want with sixty buffalo robes is beyond me."

"I'll have to pay the women, for one thing," I said. "And,

then, I'm building up a stock to start my own trading post, remember?"

"If ever a girl could do it, lassie, you're the one." Father nodded at something behind me. "Hand me that flask there. If Bedeaux's alive, he'll be needing a taste of the old Monongahela. Best cough and snakebite medicine there is."

"He isn't snakebit," I said, but I reached for the flask and the whiskey jug. "If he's alive, he's only wet and hungry, is my guess." I set them on the table and looked around for something to use as a funnel.

"Never mind that," he said. "Just you run for the food. Tell the mothers I'll have you back in ten or twelve nights."

4 July 1837

Independence Day. Left Chardon and the men toasting the health of Andrew Jackson. By the number of drinks, he should be the healthiest ex-president in history. Can't applaud his Indian policy, sorry to say. Live and let live is my motto—the Cherokee have a constitution, too. Or did have.

Took Swaggerty and my Rosalie and headed out to find Bedeaux with his wet load of robes. Air was dry and smokey. Camped in a coulee and ate cold meat and cornballs.

The girl's mothers were just as pleased to let her go as I was to have her along. She's been little use in field or lodge lately—her mind gone drifty, they say, and her tongue sharp as a blade. To that, I can testify myself. Nobody likes a rude girl, and I'm supposed to straighten her out. Fat chance—as headstrong as her mum, that child is. But she can keep the books and writes a far finer hand than myself, what with these spectacles of mine. Ben Franklin I am not.

No fire for the sake of discretion. Hostiles abroad, and we're too small a party to fight them off.

Three

As Garreau's gray mare bounced along over the short grass, the words of an old song my father taught me kept going through my mind.

> *Tam Pearce, Tam Pearce, lend me your gray mare.*
> *All along down, along out, along lea.*

I loved how the words fit perfectly with the rhythm of her trotting:

> one *two three*, trot *trot trot*
> *When shall I see again my gray mare?*
> *All along down, along trot trot–trot trot . . .*

Maybe my ancestors hummed this song as they bounced over the downs and moors in Scotland. In Scotland, they have downs and moors; here we have hills and prairies.

My father came from Scotland, so he would be a Scot, except that he changed to American when he got to Philadelphia, which is an American village. Old Frenchie

Bedeaux is French, unless he changed to Minnetaree when he got to the Knife River towns. I come from Mandan country, but since my father is Scottish, then I come from Scotland, too. The Minnetarees brought Sakakawea home from the Shoshones, near the mountains, and adopted her. But then she married Charbonneau, who is French. So her son Jean-Baptiste would be part Shoshone, part French, and part Minnetaree. It's confusing.

The men at Fort Clark say the Mandans are "Indian." And they call the Dakotas "Indian," too, and the Arikaras, and the Minnetarees, and the Crows. All "Indians." This is very annoying. These tribes are nothing alike, and they live in very different places, and they fight all the time. So how could they all be the same thing?

Up ahead, my father pointed to a small clutch of buffalo about a hundred yards away. Three young calves were chasing in and out among the cows—red calves with stiff legs and knobby knees pumping up and down. An old cow spotted us and swung heavily around. Her coat was the color of warm black earth, and it was tattered and scarred, with patches of fur coming off her flanks. I thought she looked like Swaggerty, with his holes in his shirt and his greasy buckskin trousers. She shook her head and sent a string of slobber flying. The other cows staggered up from the wallow where they were dusting themselves. They stared at us briefly, then moved off. Swaggerty said something to my father and patted his rifle, but neither of them followed the buffalo. We needed to catch up with Frenchie Bedeaux.

The first white men who came to America were Spanish hunters, looking for a place called India—which is about as far away as the moon. They saw some people and said, Oh, they must be Indians—"Indios" in Spanish.

But, see, a name is supposed to point to something, something real, as any fool would know, and the Spanish fools were not in India. So "Indian" is a name that points to nothing.

But I've said, "If you please, I am Mandan and Scottish." I've said, "There was an English princess in my family, you know." I've explained about India till I was blue in the mouth, but they just say, "Go make the fire, you silly redskin."

We dropped into a coulee and followed it for a short way, till the trail popped up and over the rim. To the southwest, a thin fog of smoke hung wide and pale blue along the high ground. The Dakotas' prairie fire. The sun was halfway down the sky in the west and was sending its yellow fingers through the haze. To the northwest, a wide bend of the river reflected the sunlight like the glass in my father's spectacles.

Muskrat Woman didn't care about what they called us. These were not Mandan words, so she thought they didn't matter. To me, they mattered. If someone called my father English, he was ready to kill, but at least English is something real. His friends called *me* Indian—which is nothing at all. How insulting! I wanted to be who I am, not some invisible made-up nothing person. White men are relatives of mine; why didn't this matter to them?

At sunset we stopped in a small wooded hollow near a stream about a mile from the river. Swaggerty hobbled the horses in the trees and let them graze while I fished corn-balls and dried meat out of the packs. We ate quietly in the dark, without a fire. About the time the coyotes began their evening chorus, the men opened the whiskey flask, and then Little Raven straggled in to flop down beside me. He had fish heads on his breath.

My father and Swaggerty talked quietly about Bedeaux and his Minnetaree wife. In the old days, some people came to the far bank of the river and said something like "min-eh-tah-ree," which means "we want to come over." That's what Muskrat Woman told me. So they're the "We Want to Come Over" people. But the Minnetarees' name for themselves is "Hidatsa" or "Awatixa," which is the name I used when I was speaking Minne— I mean, when I was speaking Hidatsa.

I wondered what the old-time Hidatsas called the Mandans. Maybe it was "They Live on the Other Side." That would be funny. And the Dakotas probably call us "River People" or "Their Corn Is Easy to Steal." And the Crows might call us "How Silly to Stay in One Place All Summer."

Indian. What a funny word, I thought sleepily. *Eeen*-juhn. *Eeen*-dyo. Ee-I-ee-I-yo. I thought I'd like to see India someday. Indie Yah. E-yah. Well, I yawned, rolling up in my blanket, I'm glad the Spanish weren't looking for a place called Turkey.

Four

～

We found Frenchie Bedeaux late in the afternoon. Or I should say Little Raven found him.

At the head of a narrow wooded island in the river, we could see where a man had dragged something heavy out of the water and into the cottonwood trees. It had to be Bedeaux, and my father motioned us to cross. Swaggerty went first with the pack horses, then I headed Garreau's gray mare into the river upstream of the island and let her swim with the current down to the near shore. My father brought up the rear. His horse huffed and blew as he clambered out of the water behind me, dripping. A short way into the trees, the remains of a small campfire were still warm, and Bedeaux's long skin-boat was upturned on a log nearby. One side of it was torn where a snag in the river had punched through, and we could tell that the old trapper had been trying to patch and brace it. A quickly made fish spear leaned against a log. About fifty yards downstream there was a sorry pile of wet buffalo robes on the bank.

"Well," said Swaggerty, taking a long look around, "at

least the old bull is still a-kicking." He swung down and began to unsaddle his horse.

"Let's see if we can locate the rest of his cargo," said my father. "Where do you figure he swamped?" The two men wandered upstream, looking for a sign, while I led the three horses toward a small clearing in the trees and picketed them. I dug my father's ledger book and a stubby pencil out of the saddlebags, laid them at the base of a tree, and started to pull apart the wet robes for counting. I grabbed the top one with both hands and peeled it away from the pile, dragging it up the bank to drape over a deadfall. Nothing in this world is heavier than a wet hide, and I want the record to show that I pulled a full dozen soaked buffalo robes up the bank of the Missouri River and draped them over logs, boulders, bent saplings—anything that might get a little air under them. I leaned against a giant cottonwood to breathe.

Directly across from the island, the main shore of the Missouri rose sharply into a cutbank that curled outward at the top and bristled with grasses, shoots, muddy twigs, and driftwood. Just over the lip of the bank, a flurry of motion caught my eye. It was a prairie chicken bursting into flight. Hardly was it airborne when the bird dropped like a stone; a half-second later, I heard the gunshot. I slipped behind my tree and started quietly back to the horses, keeping a careful eye on the far shore. I stopped short when a familiar shape burst into view. It was Little Raven, tail straight out, bounding over fallen logs and tree trash, going as fast as his three legs could take him. In his mouth was the dead prairie chicken and right behind him was Old Frenchie Bedeaux, swearing a blue streak and reloading as he ran. Little Raven dodged down the cut-bank to the shore, swung upstream, and charged into the river, the precious bird still clasped in his jaws.

Bedeaux pulled up at the lip of the bank to take aim. The barrel of the gun followed Little Raven's progress and then blossomed smoke and fire. I winced as a tiny splash nicked the river just above Little Raven. Bedeaux swore again and jumped up and down. He threw the gun down and picked up a rock. It fell far short. Another. And another. I began to grin.

Bedeaux grabbed a stick and threw that. He threw rocks, grass, twigs, whatever he could lay his hands on, stamping his feet and swearing in four different tongues. Finally he stamped in the wrong place and the cutbank caved away under him. Down he went, one foot high in the air, arms flailing, sliding through the short sky to the shore below, till he came to rest at the water's edge on his own personal landslide. There he lay, laughing like a madman and throwing clods of dirt into the air with both hands.

Five

~

I stepped into the water to steady the bull boat as Frenchie Bedeaux hopped out, and together we dragged it up the bank of the island into the low brush. He was a slender man, slightly bent, and not much taller than I. His hands were wrinkled leather, his sharp eyes deeply creased at the corners, and a short white ponytail stood out behind him. He traveled light. A buckskin bag with a beaded strap hung over one shoulder, and a powder horn on a leather cord looped across the other. He wore two simple knives at his belt, and he kept his rifle close at hand. He was a careful man, and there was not much about him that seemed lighthearted. He would not have made a good Mandan. But he nodded gruffly as we flipped the bull boat over.

"*Merci, mademoiselle*," he said.

"*De rien, monsieur*," I replied, and curtseyed in my deer-skin dress.

He snorted. "I should have known the daughter of the

professor Angus would speak the *français*." He squinted at the river's far shore and then back at me. "However, your father's accent stinks, and yours do, too."

"No one speaks French like the French," I sighed. "Except perhaps the birds."

"Ah, *c'est vrai*. It is no sound more beautiful of all the world than the voice of the nightingale or the song of the French mother." He reached down for his hunting sack. Empty, of course.

"And no one speaks *English* like the French, either," I said blandly, turning toward the path. "The honk of the giant goose or the English of a Frenchman." Bedeaux snapped his head around.

"You give me a minute," he said, cracking a smile. "I going teach you proper manners for a French girl! Right now, I am too very tired from chasing dogs." I thought I'd better wait to tell him whose dog he had been chasing.

I led Old Bedeaux through the undergrowth quietly to where Swaggerty and my father had built a fire for coffee. A roaring, crackling fire, just like in the castle in *Scott's Poetical Works*—you'd think they were roasting a whole stag, whatever that is. Swaggerty had cleared some brush for a canvas wall-tent from the fort and now he was chopping poles for it. There would be no chance of covering our traces when we left. Old Bedeaux noticed right away.

"Your relatives?" he asked. I scowled at him and walked toward the men.

"Father," I said quietly, tipping my head toward Bedeaux. He scrambled up, fumbling with his spectacles.

"So there you are, then! We heard the shot and figured you'd be bringing in supper shortly."

It was Bedeaux's turn to scowl. "*Merde alors,*" he said bitterly. "That bit of a meal was snatched by a wild dog. Snatched from my very lips." He followed this comment with a string of bitter oaths in French and Hidatsa.

"Wouldn't be a three-legged dog, would it?" Swaggerty asked with a sideways wink at me. "That one's been following us a couple days. Don't know where he came from."

"*Oui, oui!*" exclaimed Bedeaux. "The very one. I shot him in the river, but the bullet turned away at the last second. Like the magic, like the very magic!"

I couldn't help myself. "Maybe he's a medicine animal," I said. "Maybe he's a Dakota shaman spying on us. Better not to anger him." I handed Old Bedeaux a cornball and a hunk of dried buffalo from one of the packs. "We brought plenty of food," I said sweetly.

7 July 1837

Located Bedeaux and the load—swamped on a snag
near the head of an island. Out of the main channel, so
'twasn't deep, and the load traveled only a short way
till it hung on a sweeper and some other tree trash. Most
of the packs were still bound, though soaked through.
Swaggerty hitched a line to them, one pack at a time,
and I dragged them ashore by horse. Rosalie logged them
as they came in and helped me spread them and press
the water out as well as we could. Final count will be
near 500, but it will take us two more days to retrieve
them all and rebundle. It was worth the trip, even if
some 50 robes are lost. This will make me look very good to
Chardon, especially getting them with only one man.

  Bedeaux thinks he can repair the canoe. If he can,
we'll take half the robes by horse and let him float the
rest home. Still damp, they'll go twice the weight he
had in getting here.

Six

$\sim\!\!\!\sim$

While Old Bedeaux repaired the canoe, Swaggerty clawed his way out to the packs that were caught in the tree trash in the water, Father hauled them in with a horse and rope, and I unbound them to spread and dry. Dry, compared to what they were in the river, that is. I tallied them, rolled each one to squeeze out some of the water, then unrolled and counted them again as I stacked them back into bundles. It was heavy, sloppy, slippery, backbreaking work.

Deerflies and mosquitoes nibbled us constantly, and the wood ticks burrowed their little heads into the skin at the backs of our knees. The mud here wasn't as good as down by Mitutanka, but I smeared myself with it anyway to keep off most of the biting bugs. Old Bedeaux did the same. Father and Swaggerty just slapped and scratched and swore.

Swaggerty had the worst job, I think, and he was quickly as wet as the hides in the water. He had to shimmy along a forty-foot cottonwood that had fallen out into the river. Most of the packs were hung in the far branches, but some had tumbled as they hit, and those were badly stuck, held under the surface, or caught on lighter trees and deadfalls nearby. What a mess. When Swaggerty reached one he lashed a rope to it, then Father hauled it in with the horses. He wrestled the pack over to me, untied the line, and flung it back out to Swaggerty, who was swearing and thrashing and clinging for dear life to the sweep out in the river.

Frenchie Bedeaux spent his time repairing the canoe. It was a wide skin-boat, with ribs of ash and broad thwarts made of cottonwood. When the snag in the river caught the boat, a sharp branch gouged through the skin of one side, leaving a tear from one midrib to the next. As Bedeaux worked the boat off the snag, the load had shifted, and over he went. Now the job was to lace up the tear and seal it with tree sap.

Unlike Swaggerty, Old Bedeaux worked rapidly but patiently, pausing often to listen and to scan both shores of the river. He muttered to himself in French about the Dakotas chasing everyone, and then about these white men afflicting him with their help. Muskrat Woman told me once that Bedeaux had been away from his kind so long, he had forgotten he was a white man himself.

Seven

*N*o one ever sees the Dakotas coming. Not really.

I had started a small morning fire from the embers of the night before, our fifth night out. I was on my knees with my face down near the fire, blowing gently along the base of a stick where the coals glowed pink under a layer of gray. A tiny flame and a wisp of smoke came up toward my eyes as I pulled back for a breath of air.

In front of the tent he shared with Swaggerty, my father stood frowning, deep in his morning ritual. Holding his spectacles gently by the ear wires, he puffed explosively at each round lens, then rubbed them on his tongue and smeared them on the least muddy square of his shirttail. Then he scowled through the glass and repeated the process. Old Bedeaux sat several yards to one side with his back to a cottonwood, sipping quietly from a tin cup of coffee. Behind me lay a fallen tree, its roots and branches framing a hollow that might have been a bear's den last winter.

The sun had just begun to push its morning beams toward us through the mist and trees. The river's gurgle, so loud in the night, was now a murmur at the edge of my attention. For a long moment, even the sparrows were still, and the only sound was the drizzle of Swaggerty emptying the coffeepot in the weeds behind the tent.

Then Little Raven's ears went up. Quietly he rose to his feet, every sense alert. The hair on the back of my neck began to prickle. I glanced nervously at Bedeaux, and he was watching the dog, too. He set his cup aside carefully and reached for the flintlock leaning beside him. Holding my breath, I slid slowly toward the fallen tree.

"*Merde!*" said Bedeaux suddenly. He rolled to his left, taking the gun with him in one smooth motion. A sound like a cannon went off somewhere to my right, and a hole appeared in the tree where Bedeaux's head had just been resting. With a scream, I dived into the hollow under the deadfall as what seemed like a dozen voices tore the air. Swaggerty yelped once and crashed into the tent, tangled with a Dakota raider. Another Dakota, streaked in paint and mud, leapt the fire. He swung a trader's iron tomahawk as he launched himself at my father. I stifled another scream.

Angus, still fixing his spectacles to his ears, sidestepped neatly as the man flew by. He snatched the new horse pistol from his belt. It blew fire and smoke as he shot the fellow rising from the ground. Flipping the gun, he grabbed the barrel and brought the grip down like a war club against the head of the raider who had hold of Swaggerty.

"Up, Swaggerty!" my father shouted. "Rosalie, Bedeaux, to me! We'll make a stand by the horses!"

From nearby, Bedeaux's rifle spoke, and the old man's voice followed, swearing. "*Non, non,* you fool English!" he called. "You stay together, they kill you together!" My father had found his rifle now, and he fired a shot into the trees. He crouched behind a cottonwood to reload.

"Don't call me English, you daft old Papist!"

There was a splash, but we heard nothing more from the old man. Two more shots exploded; a horse screamed. My father was shouting and Swaggerty swearing while Dakota voices yelled in their own tongue. I made myself small and shrank low into the hollow under the tree.

11 July 1837—Writing this in the near dark.

Dakotas ambushed the island. We dispatched four and the rest retreated with most of our horses. Swaggerty is killed, Bedeaux presumed drowned, and my poor Rosalie disappeared. Captured or slain, I know not which, and one about as dire as the other. I found no body, so may God have mercy on her, alive or dead. I blame myself— would ne'er have brought her, save for my failing eyes.

Caught Garreau's mare running loose at the head of the island. Packed only my necessaries and left the load of robes where they lay. Should travel by night to evade pursuit and sleep days in the coulees. If the smoke thickens, however, will brave it for daytime travel.

Eight

"Last Child! Here!" A brown hand reached down into my hiding place and grabbed me by the wrist. It was Young Wolf. I jumped up and he dragged me toward the trees.

"What are you doing here?" I demanded.

"No time to talk," he answered. "Run! My horse is this way!" I crouched low and dodged through the underbrush while Young Wolf pounded along ahead of me.

"Be careful," I whispered angrily. "There must be a dozen of them!"

"Only six," he shouted back. "Or maybe two now." When I reached the horse, Young Wolf was already untying it. He hoisted me to its back and threw himself aboard behind me.

"If there are only two, then we should go back and help Father!" I panted.

"Old Short-Eyes will make it," Young Wolf replied. "I cut his horse loose and told him to meet us downriver."

I twisted round to look at him. "You're kidding. Angus can't read sign; he'll never find us."

"Then he'll meet us at the village," he said tersely, kicking the horse in the ribs. The sound of gunshots followed us briefly, but soon the noise of the fight was washed away in the fresh morning air. We trotted half a mile down the bank and crossed the channel to the western shore of the river. I could see the tracks of the Dakota horses where they had come down the bank and entered the water this morning. Young Wolf's horse clambered up to a notch and humped his way over the top. Here was more sign of the Dakotas: horse tracks and the prints of Dakota moccasins with their rounded toe. I saw what looked like a boot track, too, but Young Wolf urged the horse onward before I could be sure. We seemed to be tracking them backward.

"Won't they come back this way, too?" I asked. Young Wolf laughed, but he seemed tense, as if he was afraid of the same thing.

"Nah," he said. "Dakotas never take the same way twice. You know that."

As we left the trees and rode up the swells of the prairie, the smoke became heavier. We could see well enough, but not far enough, and the air was heavy with the sweet scent of burning grasses. We passed several small herds of buffalo cows and calves moving west and north as we traveled southward.

"Maybe the buffalo are telling us something," I suggested. Young Wolf shrugged.

"Maybe we should shoot one," he said. "It might be a long while till we eat again."

"We can go without. It's only three days to Fort Clark."

For some reason, we were taking the western side of the

river. Swaggerty and my father had chosen the eastern side in coming up to find Old Bedeaux, deliberately to avoid the smoke. Then something dawned on me.

"This can't be the Dakotas' fire," I said to Young Wolf. "We're too far north."

He grunted. "It's a Dakota fire, all right. There hasn't been any lightning since the new moon." And he wouldn't say any more about it. He handed me a skin of water. "Have a sip. That's all you get for a while." The water was warm but welcome as it slid down my throat. My eyes itched and my lungs had begun to feel ragged, as if I'd been screaming. We needed a brisk wind to clear the air.

Young Wolf didn't drink the water, but he pulled a small gourd from somewhere and shook it beside his ear. Empty. With a disgusted face, he unstoppered it and sucked angrily. I caught the faint smell of whiskey, and it brought my father's voice to mind: "Don't let me catch you with that stuff on your breath." Angus believed women's blood couldn't handle strong drink; he thought it turned them into drunkards quicker than it did with men. "You don't want to end up like those sad women begging round the fort for a drink with Swaggerty and Garreau." Young Wolf hung around the fort a good bit, too, I thought, and more than once I'd seen him passed out by the gate in the morning, unable to make it home after a night of drinking with the white men. I sat still, squinting over the horse's head into the smoke.

"How long till we're past the smoke?" I asked.

"Stop whining!" he snapped. He bumped the horse

sharply with his heels and we lurched forward. I thought about jumping off, or at least throwing an elbow into his ribs, but then he softened his tone. "There's a nice deep coulee about half a day from here," he said. "We should be clear of it then, or, if not, we can hole up there till it blows over." We kept on. "Besides," he added, "this way the Dakotas won't follow us."

It wasn't blowing over. In fact, it was blowing toward us. Soon, the scent of burning grass didn't seem sweet to me anymore; it was harsh and bitter. And the smoke was getting thick now, lying along the ground like a poison fog. The more I rubbed my eyes, the more they burned. I could feel the horse begin to tremble between my knees, and his breath came in heavy wheezes. I wished desperately for something to cover my nose and mouth, but there was nothing. Instead, I hunched my neck and tucked my face inside the collar of my dress. Young Wolf was coughing, but he urged the horse onward. We should go east, down to the river, I thought. It's only a couple of miles. The river would keep us safe. I closed my eyes and breathed shallow breaths into my collar.

The coulee came on us abruptly at midday. I saw only the top few leaves of an ash tree, and then we dropped sharply into shelter. The sides of the coulee were steep and thick with short willow, ash, and cranberry. This must be a wet place in the spring, I thought. Sadly, the smoke was only a little lighter.

"This is not going to work for long," I told Young Wolf, coughing. "We need to get to the river."

"Wolf Boy," came a mild voice, "your fire done cut us off from the river." I spun around.

A white man was slouching comfortably at the base of a young ash. The steamboat captain! "Only way out is the way you come in," he said. "So that's the way we'll go . . . maybe tomorrow." He stood up and walked toward us, smiling. His white coat had gone gray, and dirty yellow whiskers had sprouted across his chin.

"What about the others?" said Young Wolf, swinging down from the horse.

"What others?" I asked.

"Why, the boys from the island, of course," replied the captain. "Didn't Young Wolf tell you his little secret? He's thrown in with bad company." He giggled stupidly behind his broken teeth.

I turned to face Young Wolf. "What's he talking about?" I demanded. "The Dakotas?" Young Wolf looked away. "You raided us with Dakotas?"

"Oh, who cares about them?" said the captain pleasantly. "They'll meet us, or they'll miss us in the smoke. No difference, really, now that we got what we were after. You done good, Wolf Boy. Real good." He was smiling broadly under the flat brim of his hat. "And you know how nice I can be to real good Injuns, don't you?" He dangled a flat-sided bottle from his fingers, waved it gently in Young Wolf's direction. The whiskey made a sound in the glass like pure, clean water polishing the smoothest stones in the world.

13 July 1837

Made it back to Ft. Clark last night at a dead run,
with two Dakota warriors in pursuit. Bless Garreau's
little gray mare, she ran her heart out. Medicine Bird
and a handful of Mandan warriors charged off in
pursuit of the Dakotas, but came back empty soon
after. Too dark, they said.

This morning I begged Chardon to commission a
search party for Rosalie. The toad—he says he will not.
Too many days have passed since she disappeared, and
most of the men are out after buffalo to the east. If it
were his child, his precious Andrew Jackson Chardon,
we'd spare no expense. Mine are a penny a dozen.

Though it break my heart, it must be said she could
be anywhere by now. Had to give this sad news to
Rosalie's mothers. Goes to Next Timber was beside herself
and would not speak to me. White Crane, equally hys-
terical, couldn't <u>stop</u> talking—or, rather, threatening.
The sisters take their cue from the mothers, and both hold
me responsible. With not even that dunce Young Wolf to
stop round, it is a lodge full of women. It's hardly my
fault we were attacked by the Dakotas, but I expect
nonetheless to find my boots outside the lodge at any time.

Nine

I lay curled like a child. My feet were tied to a small ash tree and my hands tied to a long cord, the other end of which was looped around Young Wolf's wrist. I couldn't have gone very far in the smoke, even if I'd been able to get free, but I guess they didn't want to chase me. What would they do with me later? I was furious and terrified by turns, and resting was impossible. I passed the night trying to keep Young Wolf miserable. Whenever he drifted into sleep, I jerked on the cord. Twice, I sent him sprawling as he reached for his whiskey.

At daybreak, they untied me. I was rubbing my ankles when a buffalo cow, escaping the smoke on the prairie above, wandered into our coulee. Her eyes bulged wide and white when she saw us. She didn't want to be so close to people, but she wasn't climbing back into the smoke, either. She blew hard through both nostrils, stamped and turned and tossed her head, as if she were searching for something. But the captain gave her no time to decide; he raised his rifle and shot her through the heart. She took one backward step, sat down, and flopped to her side. A chill went down my back as she died staring right at me.

"Well, the Lord provided a cow in a thicket," said the captain with a chuckle. "Too bad we can't build a fire to make a burnt sacrifice." He laughed out loud. "Wouldn't want to start a fire, would we, Wolfie?"

Young Wolf the Good Injun laughed, too, though he wasn't following this. He was already stupid with drink this morning.

"Cow in a thicket," the captain prompted cheerfully. "You like them Bible stories, girlie?" he asked me. "Your daddy read 'em to you, does he?"

"He reads them," I declared. "I don't like them. That white god kills too many children—did you ever notice that?" I stood up and stretched my back. "All those first-born in Egypt. All those wandering in the wilderness. And there's hardly a pair of twins he'll leave alone. Look at Cain and Abel. Look at Jacob and Esau."

The captain started. "What?" he said, his voice hollow all of a sudden.

"Nothing," I answered. "It's just that he chooses one over the other." The captain's face went dark. "Or look at Job," I went on. "He makes a bet with the devil and poor old Job has to pay the price. Doesn't seem right." I had found a sore spot with the captain, which pleased me greatly. I pressed a little. "What's the trouble? You like those stories?"

"Doesn't matter," he said tersely. He turned his back and circled the cow slowly.

"Come on," I teased. "What's your favorite? Did you like Job? Disgusting open sores all over him like smallpox, and his last child runs in to say the family's all dead. 'I only am escaped alone to tell thee.' You like that one? I have to say, the Lord doesn't look so good there."

"You shouldn't make light of the Scriptures."

"But what's your favorite? Come on."

"You shouldn't make light . . ."

"I bet you like Jacob and Esau. Why does he choose Jacob, anyway? 'Jacob have I loved,' and all that."

"Stop it."

"But why would he choose Jacob? Jacob was a terrible hunter; Esau was great. It makes no sense."

"Shut up!" he shouted. "Shut up! You say one more word about Jacob and I swear I'll cut your tongue out!" The captain's face was bright red under his yellow hair, and his eyes stood out bloodshot and unblinking. I turned away to gnaw a hunk of pemmican, silent but enjoying the moment.

Young Wolf was not in the mood to be serious. He started singing aloud. He danced over to me, making faces, trying to be my best friend in the world. The pouch around his neck swung freely back and forth. "Get away," I told him crossly. "I don't even know you."

"Oh, don't be so cross," he teased. "That was a good trick we played on Old Short-Eyes. Shot up the camp and snatched you right from under his nose. Right from under his . . . spectacles!" Oh, that was a funny one. Short-Eyes. His spectacles. He laughed a good long time about that. Ho-ho-ho.

"Hey," he said, poking me with a knuckle. "Hey. Wasn't that a good trick? Wasn't it? And now he'll have to pay to get you back. Heh-heh-heh." Poor drunken fool couldn't stop chuckling.

It was driving me crazy. I yelled at the captain, "Is that what this is about? Ransom? If you think you can get money out of a bookkeeper at a fur-company outpost, then you're a bigger fool than Young Wolf."

The captain didn't answer. "Wolf Boy," he said, "come here and give me a hand with this." He had opened the buffalo's belly and pulled her tangled insides onto the ground. He found her liver and took a huge bite before tossing it away. He was skinning her now, standing near the knee-deep pile of green-and-purple guts.

This was the white way, I had learned. The Mandans treated each buffalo as a gift, used every part for its right purpose. But the whites wanted only the meat and the hide. With copper pans and garden hoes made of steel, who needs a bladder and a shoulder blade?

Young Wolf went over to help, weaving on his feet and humming happily. "They say that the women are cursing the men, eyah . . ."

"Here," said the captain, "make yourself useful." He handed Young Wolf a skinning knife with a wide curved blade and a wooden handle. "I'll pull the hide, and you stroke it down close there. And don't mess it up. I'd make the little squaw do it, but we can't trust her with a knife." He took hold of the limp hide with both hands and pulled it tight while Young Wolf worked the blade in small arcs close between the hide and body. The knife made quiet tearing sounds as it sliced through tissue.

"It ain't about money," said the captain suddenly. His face was calm again; a smear of blood ran from one corner of his mouth to his ear. "There's nobody takes a potshot at Tom Hatcher and lives to laugh about it."

"Hatcher?" I said, confused. "I thought you were Captain Pratte from the fur company."

"Young Captain Pratte . . ." he said, yanking the hide hard. "Now, there's the only pure fool I've seen on the river. He's even dumber than Wolf Boy here." He snorted. "Putting on airs till me and the crew all hated his guts, and this on his first trip up the river. Then he goes off to dance with the village Injuns, leaving us on the steamboat. Hah. Showed him. And I'll show your pa, too." He spat on the ground and tugged again at the heavy hide. "Mind the blade there, boy. You've nicked the robe."

Young Wolf was humming again, as drunk and happy as I'd ever seen him. The curved knife seemed to fly in his hand to the rhythm of his song. His arms and legs were covered in blood, and he had put one foot down for balance into the open chest of the buffalo's big carcass. It looked like he was chopping his way out of a monster cocoon on the first day of spring. If I hadn't hated him from the soles of my feet upward, I'd have laughed. I looked away, thinking about what the captain—I mean Tom Hatcher—had said.

"Well, if it isn't about money, what is it about? What on earth do you expect to get by kidnapping me?" I asked.

He looked up at me again, but his eyes were having trouble focusing. His ragged mouth twitched. "I want it all," he growled. "I want his horse, his traps, his books, his writing tools, his spectacles." Hatcher looked around the coulee for more ideas. "I want his pride. I want him to know fear. I want him naked and begging for mercy just before I cut his heart out."

He meant it. A cold trickle of sweat slid down my ribs.

"His knife, too," added Young Wolf.

"What?" said Hatcher.

"A knife for a knife." Young Wolf was grinning stupidly. "For the balance."

A completely crazy smile spread across the white man's face. "Yes, that's it," he said. "I want his knife. And his shiny new pistol."

I looked at these two men: one happy fool with a knife and a whiskey bottle, and one genuine lunatic up to his eyes in religion and revenge. I breathed slowly, calming not fear so much as anger. I knew I should be afraid. I even tried to be afraid. But what I felt was a cold rage against these two pitiful, dangerous, stupid men who somehow had taken control of my life. I stood up and changed the subject.

"Do you ever get headaches?" I said to Tom Hatcher. He was tugging on the buffalo hide again, while Young Wolf was singing and working the knife. Hatcher grunted.

"Get 'em all the time," he said, not looking up.

"Have you tried chewing willow bark?"

"Not lately."

"You should try it. Muskrat plant, too," I said. I nodded down the coulee behind him. "You should send Drunk Wolf down there to cut some willow for you."

He glanced at Young Wolf. When he turned to search the coulee for willows, I picked up a heavy stick and swung it as hard as I could against the side of Young Wolf's head. Oh, that felt good. He dropped like a tree, and I hit him again. He tried to roll away, but I stayed after him, pounding him with the stick, hitting any part of him I could reach. Tom Hatcher stood watching—too surprised to interfere.

"You drunken, wretched, worthless traitor," I shouted, whacking him with every word. "Sold me out for a drink of whiskey!" Young Wolf tried to get up, but he was too drunk. I hit him in the butt, the back of the head, the shoulder. "You make me vomit! Raiding with Dakotas! Worthless, stinking, white man's rat!"

My stick broke, so I threw it away and started with my hands. I grabbed a fistful of hair and jerked his head back. I punched him in the mouth. I bit his ear. I tore the pouch from around his neck and threw it to the ground. I scratched his face. "I'm going to pluck your eyes and make you eat them! Go marry a buzzard! You'll never sleep in our lodge again!"

I beat him till I was too tired to raise my arm. Finally, I sat down, panting. Young Wolf lay on his back, coughing and touching his puffy lip with his fingers. I was too small to hurt him much, but at least he wasn't singing anymore.

14 July 1837

Sky today very smokey as the Dakotas' fire
draws closer.

Tried again to get up a search party to look
for R. Tried the Mandans this time, but they
wouldn't go either. Even Medicine Bird, generally
a good friend, says the trail is cold. And there was
some backtalk that a rude white girl wasn't much
worth saving—an argument at which not only
I but her mothers, too, took umbrage. Still, it seems
our Rosalie has a sharper tongue and fewer friends
than I would have expected. I know her sharp
tongue, but, my God, what a terrible fate for such a
small sin.

I suspect the greater reason is that the Mandans
hold the whites responsible for the smallpox. They don't
know how, but they know it came from the steamboat. An alarming many of them show full-blown
symptoms, and the first one died today. Even the chief
Matoh-Topa—The Four Bears—has the unmistakable
fever, pains in the belly, great sorrow.

I know how it came from the steamboat—in the
blankets, and then man to man—but so far no one
cares for my advice to move all the sick to one big lodge
and keep others away. They can't get around their own
idea that sickness is conveyed by spirits. In a quarrel
about blankets, only the crazy old grandmother,

Muskrat Woman, took my side. "White sickness, white ways," she said, if I translate aright. Well put, and thank you, dear old lady. But I still lost the argument. No crude white man could possibly know how to cure an honest Mandan.

Ten

Riding facedown across the back of a horse isn't so bad when you get used to it. At least with my head down there I couldn't hear Young Wolf singing. All I could hear was the snorting of the horses and the muffled clopping of their hooves. And the view was better down low, too. Only the short-grass prairie going by in front of my nose. I didn't have to look at the shifty-eyed face of Tom Hatcher or Young Wolf's whiskey grin. It's true that, being doubled over like that, I couldn't get a good breath, and my face was going numb, and my nose was running, and I was getting dizzy. And with my hands tied to my feet by a loop running under the belly of the horse, I was afraid of slipping under and being trampled. Still, not so bad. A small price to pay.

Young Wolf stopped humming for a moment. He coughed from the smoke he was breathing up there above the horse and looked down at me.

"You think you're better than everyone," he muttered angrily.

"I *am* better than *you*," I muttered. "You're a greedy,

drunken, double-crossing piece of dog meat." I tried to spit on the ground, but that's not so easy when you're hanging upside down.

"Who cares?" he answered. "I don't think you're a clan member. You're half white. I don't think you're even a Mandan. Just red on the outside; all white on the inside. That's what you said—you're one of the white people from the fort. You can read the talking papers. You can speak their language. You want to be white so bad? Fine, then, be white. See what it gets you."

"What you think doesn't matter, Whiskey Boy," I said coldly. "Dakota Boy. You're dead to me. You're dead to the whole lodge."

But his words stung me badly. Being part white made Tom Hatcher think I was worth kidnapping. It made Young Wolf willing to sell me out, as if I wasn't even a Mandan. Knowing the white man's numbers made my father take me out to find Frenchie Bedeaux, instead of leaving me at home to tend the crops, where a proper Mandan woman would have been. My heart began to hurt, and my eyes were watering. I told myself it was from the smoke.

Who was I becoming? All the times that White Crane had spoken sharply, all the times Muskrat Woman had looked at me strangely, all the names I had ever been called—they all came back to me in that moment as I hung over the back of the horse. In that moment, I knew it was all because I was white on the inside. White like my father.

White like Tom Hatcher. Whiteness made me pushy and angry. Made me greedy and impatient. That's why they all hated me. Whiteness. I hated it myself. If I could find the white part of me, I would tear it out with my teeth.

I calmed my breathing. All I needed was a plan. I wasn't going to be white anymore, that was the first thing. Beating Young Wolf with a stick was actually a very promising start. No white woman would have done that. Good. The second thing was to trick these men—and I knew that would take a Mandan woman, too.

In the coulee, when I had finished pounding on Young Wolf, I had sat down on the pouch I'd torn off him. Inside was his little flint knife, the one he'd tried to trade for a cup of whiskey. That knife was hiding right now in my left fist, waiting to be useful. I whispered to it softly. "Where's the best place to cut? Maybe cut the line to my feet. No? Here, between my wrists? Yes, better." The little blade was sharp. Flint is a gift from Lone Man, I'm sure. Slowly the blade slid out between the heels of my hands, and I began to saw the leather thong that Tom Hatcher had tied at my wrists while my mind worked on the next step.

The smoke was thick all around. We had left the coulee when Tom Hatcher could see the fire maybe half a mile from the rim. Lunatics either love a fire or fear it, my father says, and I guess Hatcher was the fearful kind. In a way, that was all I needed to know. He was coughing now, and standing in his stirrups looking back toward the south, the way we'd come. Not that there was much to see—he was only hoping we were going in the right direction. He pulled up and spoke to Young Wolf.

"Is the river still that way?"

"Yes, but still cut off by fire." Tom Hatcher's horse tossed its head and danced sideways. Now was the time, I decided, and the little flint blade popped through the thong.

"Hey!" shouted Hatcher. "She's loose!" Too bad, I thought. You've lost your little white captive, and now you've got to deal with a Mandan woman.

I slid off the horse, and as my hands passed over its rump, I slashed it hard with the little flint blade. The poor beast squealed and leapt sideways, crunching Tom Hatcher's leg. Hatcher's own horse reared, struck out with a forefoot. Both of them charged away into the smoke with Hatcher and Young Wolf holding on for dear life.

Eleven

I jumped clear of the horse and fell flat. I'd forgotten that my feet were tied. Feverishly, I worked at the ties with my little knife while the drumming of the horses' hooves faded into the distance, slowed, and then grew louder again. The thong between my ankles began to shred under the stone blade. I strained against them. For some reason, the horses stopped. I could hear Tom Hatcher coughing and swearing only yards away, but I couldn't see him through the smoke. Good. That meant he couldn't see me, either. The ties around one ankle snapped, and I stood up to run. But which way? I squatted down again. The horses were circling, staying close together so as not to lose each other in the smoke. I knew Young Wolf was leaning down to read the ground for my tracks. But he wouldn't be as determined as I was.

Close to the ground, the air was much better. I crouched for a breath, then stood again to consider directions. Maybe the river. But it would be miles away, and we were cut off from it by the fire. The only sure way to go was back toward the coulee, following the horses' tracks. Trouble was, that direction was also toward the fire. It could easily be moving up the coulee itself by now. Doubts were stalling me. My eyes streamed from the smoke and frustration.

I wished I could toss my eyes upward like Coyote, up above the smoke, where I could look around. I would never throw them more than four times like Coyote. Grandmother Mouse and Buffalo would never have to lend me their eyes.

I bent for another breath. Buffalo eyes. The buffalo that Tom Hatcher had shot in the coulee—how directly she had looked at me as she blew out her last breath. What was she trying to say? I stared down at the horse tracks, and then I began to run, following them back toward the coulee.

The smoke and heat grew thicker with every yard. My eyes stung. My skin prickled as the smoke dusted me with warm, filthy ash. My lungs were quickly tired of breathing poison, and they made me stop often to kneel and gasp in the cleaner air near the ground. I took to holding my breath while I ran, then pausing every twenty strides to bend down, cough, and gulp another breath. It was slow progress.

Behind me, I heard Young Wolf shout. He must have found a footprint. I cut left, angling away from the horses' trail, deliberately gouging a mark where I turned. I followed the line of a low rise through the short grass and turned again, stamping a half-dozen footprints toward the river. A hundred steps later, I very carefully swung again, counting my steps back toward the horse tracks. I could only hope that Young Wolf would fall for my trick. Even soaked in whiskey he was a Mandan hunter, not a foolish white boatman. I hated him, but as a Mandan I was proud of his skill.

I felt the fire more than saw it as I gained on the coulee. The air was scorching, and the smoke rolled along the ground in fat clouds of blue and black and gray. Blisters were swelling on my arms where flying cinders had struck me. I knew I shouldn't stop, but a fit of choking threw me to the ground. I lay still for a moment, thinking nothing, trying only to suck in some small mouthful of air.

My ear, pressed to the ground, picked up the thumping of horse hooves. Young Wolf must have figured me out. My heart almost stopped. But the hoofbeats were rough and irregular, as if the horses were revolting. They didn't want to go any closer to the fire, and I knew their lungs would be burning worse than mine. A lot of commotion, and then the hooves began drumming their regular rhythm again—moving away at a gallop. I collapsed on the sweet green grass to breathe.

I began to crawl, feeling more than seeing the horse tracks that led toward the coulee. In a few yards, my fingers and knees found the game trail we had taken before. I took a deep breath through a handful of grass and struggled to my feet again. Now I could see what the horses had seen, and I froze like a rabbit in plain sight. Directly to my right, leaping streaks of orange and crimson, feathers of black smoke, crowded toward me. Ahead, the fire had filled the lower end of the coulee like a river leaving its banks, and it was quickly flooding upward.

I crouched and dropped over the side of the coulee. Holding my hands over my mouth and nose, I staggered downslope till I picked out the large dark mound on the ground to my left. The buffalo, half butchered, lay where Tom Hatcher had left her.

I threw myself down and burrowed under the bloody hide as the fire washed over us.

PART THREE

The River

15 July 1837

A quiet day. Hunting party came in with news of a good kill to the east. Sent men with horses and a party of women to bring back the meat and robes. Smoke very heavy, difficult to see as far as the hills. A fine time for horse thieves.

Still no sign of R., my wee waif. Can't bring myself even to write her name. There's little chance she escaped the Dakotas or the fires, but one must ne'er give up hope.

White Crane blames me as much as I blame myself. She alternates between suicidal thoughts and thoughts of murdering me in my sleep. Goes to Next Timber prevents her from acting on either. I may take to sleeping in the fort.

One

⌒

*I*n my dreams, I heard the voice of Muskrat Woman telling stories on winter nights. As the fire burned low, the only sound beyond her voice was the creaking of cottonwood trees outside in the cold.

Lone Man was going along and he saw Buffalo tending a green plant. Buffalo told him it was tobacco. Buffalo sent him to Ear-on-Fire, who taught him to make a spark by striking two flint rocks together. This is how Lone Man learned to light his tobacco for the ceremonies. In thanks, Lone Man said the Mandans must have a buffalo in every ceremony.

I woke shivering. Under the hide, I hunched and trembled like a duckling in a dark egg. On my cheeks, my hands felt so cold they made me flinch. I pushed myself back into sleep, clutching the smokey fur.

Again stories flowed through me. The woman who married a buffalo; the boy who became a bear. I drifted deep into stories and found something there, surrounded by my animal relatives, that I didn't want to leave. The antelope woman never came back to being human, and neither would I. I would shed my body like a split cocoon, and I would live with the buffalo forever.

It was hunger that woke me the next time. How annoying to find that I was no buffalo after all. Not even a butterfly— only a toasted caterpillar trapped in her cocoon.

There was a cramp in my neck, and three large blisters on my arm felt as if they were still on fire. I blew an ant from my upper lip, which made me realize there was another one on my ankle, and another in my hair. Always the first workers after a fire, the ants seemed to be crawling over every inch of me. That was good, I decided. It meant I could feel.

Cautiously, I stretched, and a scorched-earth smell slid under the lip of my shelter. With it, the scent of charred meat came like a taunting whisper. I was so hungry.

I unclenched my fingers one by one and brought them up near my face. They held the little flint knife. In my other hand was a fierce fistful of buffalo hair. I whispered thanks to Lone Man and to Buffalo, for the cow who came to be killed by Tom Hatcher, and I promised to make them a gift one day. Gently, I flexed all my joints before I rolled to my knees and untucked the hide from around me.

Fresh, cool air. I knew how green the coulee should smell on a bright midsummer day, but the sour scent around me told a different story. I opened my eyes to look.

Under a blue sky, the coulee ran away on all sides in

shades of charcoal and ash. A shred of gray smoke drifted loosely up the hill. The only spots of color were pale lines of pink embers still smoldering in the blackened trunks of trees.

I looked up to see a buzzard circling forty feet above me. Ragged black unmoving wings behind a tender pink head and a face as wrinkled as a baby's. Well, I thought, he has other choices. I gathered my few wits and set to work.

The fire had left a thick char over the carcass of my buffalo. With my little knife, I scraped and cut and tore until I came away with a handful, half black and half raw, from the cow's meaty hump. I sucked it for the juices, swallowed, and bent double in a coughing fit. This would take a while.

16 July 1837

Fires have abated for the moment or, one hopes, for good. No news in any quarter but the smallpox. There is a constant drumming and singing, as the poor Indian folk wait upon their gods to save them.

Two more deaths in Mitutanka, and there's news of many with symptoms in the Little Village. It may take some time to weather this disease. If experience in the East is any teacher, the Indians are almost defenseless to it.

Word came while I was away that our steamboat captain was not young Captain Pratte, as we supposed. A mutiny among the crew had put off Captain Pratte downstream, and the boat when it passed through Ft. Clark was under command of a man, Hatcher, known to be dangerous and unstable. Young Pratte later commandeered a Mackinaw boat and hopes to overtake the pirates west of Ft. Union. Godspeed to him, though I think he won't have speed enough to catch them before they disperse into the wilderness.

Two

My father always said adventures only happen when someone is stupid or unprepared. I didn't know what he'd say about the cause of my little adventure with Young Wolf and the fire, but I was determined not to have another one before I got back to Mitutanka. And I was determined to get back.

How to get back was the question. And how to get started immediately. I figured that somewhere right now Tom Hatcher and Young Wolf were crawling out of whatever hole they'd slithered into, and that they'd be back here to pick up my trail as soon as ever they could. It was lucky for me that Tom Hatcher, being a lunatic, was just as afraid of the fire as his horse was. A little more luck to *keep* him nervous was all I asked. Nervous and slow. I was a bit jumpy myself when I thought about it, but I didn't dare to be slow.

I looked over my inventory. I had one dead buffalo, one buffalo hide, one pile of buffalo guts—all rather scorched, but still good for food and shelter if one were planning to stay. I had one little flint knife. One small coulee, with trees lightly burnt, and grasses the color of gunpowder, which went *crunch-*

crunch wherever I stepped. I had the morning sun climbing higher into the sky, and the hope of about one full day to get out of here. All in all, not too promising. On the other hand, hope is more of an attitude than a promise, and I didn't see any promise at all in giving up hope. That was so much like something Muskrat Woman would say, my eyes went all blurry. Where was my grandmother when I needed her?

I knew what she would say about this adventure. She'd say it was greed and stupidity—Angus's own stupidity—that caused it. Being greedy causes all kinds of trouble—that's in more stories than I can count. He was supposed to be so all-fired smart, with his talking papers and his spectacles and all. Hadn't he heard about Coyote—all the trouble his greed and foolishness causes everyone? Then why did Angus take only one man and one girl on an outing like this when he knew there were Dakotas around? Thought nothing would happen to him. Thought he could get all the buffalo robes himself. Big, smart, white man. Look where his big ideas have left me.

No use thinking about that, I decided. I would only get angry, and that would interfere with scheming. Also, some small part of me was being careful not to think about what might have happened to Angus. There was no telling whether he left the island alive, and the idea of him dead was something I couldn't allow into my mind. I resolved to think only about getting back to Mitutanka.

It shouldn't take much, Grandmother would say. All I needed was a boat and a river. I knew roughly where to find the river: out the end of the coulee and over the prairie toward the morning sun. It shouldn't be far—half a day of walking at most. But there wasn't a boat in sight, and I didn't expect to find one at the river. I tore out another handful of buffalo hump and sucked it. I needed water for drinking, too, I thought, as I chewed the smokey meat.

At the river, maybe I could find enough driftwood to make a raft, a small one, lashed together with roots and willow bark. But, no, drift logs don't come in matched sizes, and you can't saw them with a little flint blade.

I let my mind drift while I watched the buzzard patiently waiting in the sky. He'd been joined by a partner, and they were both floating, circling, hoping their simple buzzard hopes. I could just imagine one perched here on the buffalo's hump and the other sinking his head into the pile of guts. They'd soon have helpers, too. Mice and flies and little birds. Maybe a coyote. Within a few days, there would be little left of the buffalo. That's the way of things. In the white religion, there are spirits with white wings, angels, who come to gather the dead people and lead them to the next world. Angels must be like buzzards, I thought. They wait gently for the right moment to raise us up and give us wings.

I didn't mind sharing the meat, but it seemed a shame to leave a good hide for them to make holes in. Buffalo hides are so useful: you can make clothes, and bedding, and so many things out of them. Things like . . . I sat up straight.

Things like a small boat.

My supplies looked much different to me now. Among

the trees, I found two short saplings, dead from last winter. They were charred but sturdy, and they broke off near the ground with only a moment of wrestling. At the bottom of the pile of guts were yards and yards of undamaged intestine. I untangled the skinniest parts, hacked off four lengths, and squeezed out the slime onto the filthy ground.

The bloody side of the hide had held up well in the fire. Rolling up in it during a prairie fire is not how I was taught to tan a hide, but I wasn't here to quibble. I flopped it in thirds, rolled it, and lashed it crosswise to the charred poles with my wet gut ropes. I could never carry the hide as far as the river, but on a travois, I was sure I could drag it that far.

I sawed fist-sized hunks of meat from the bones and tucked them into the package. Nothing lifts my spirits like plain work. I heard something and jerked around. It was only myself, humming happily. "They say that the women are worse than the men. . . ."

When I find the river, I told myself, the first thing I'll do is wash the soot and blood from my body and chew up some willow bark to ease my blisters. They burned constantly. After a last bite and a wave to the buzzards, I seized the ends of the two poles and started down the coulee, dragging my new inventory behind me. The track I was leaving would be visible from half a mile away, but there was no helping that. Tom Hatcher would know that I'd try for the river anyway, as soon as he figured out I was still alive.

"And I am alive," I said through gritted teeth. "I am still alive."

17 July 1837

I have given up all hope of raising a search party from either the Mandans or Ft. Clark. Am forbidden by Mr. Chardon to go out and track her alone.

Distracting myself with events here hardly eases the pain in my chest. Foodstuffs are growing short, and no buffalo in the vicinity. Men in the fort are assigned to cutting and stacking hay, and to woodcutting. Others hunting to the east.

The Mandans are starving as well. They do without anyway from time to time, and bravely so, but now things are especially grim, as they have let the farms go to ruin while so many women are down with the sickness. Ten more dead in the village, and ever more fall with the signs of it. Tempers are short, the mood is ugly. Young men boast and call for war upon Ft. Clark. Chardon says let them come and get it over with. We've patch and powder enough to hold off a regiment.

Three

In my clan, there was a story of a young woman who had been taken from the Pawnees and was brought to Mitutanka as a young girl—like Sakakawea had come from the Shoshones to the Minnetarees. Her new family treated her well, but she always wanted to go home, to her own village in the south. When her husband rode off with The Black Cat to fight the Cheyenne and didn't come back all summer, she decided it was time to leave. She took a backpack, a bull boat, and her baby, and she paddled and poled and walked her way home. It took her almost a month. Her husband went after her, of course, and she agreed to come back with him. But think of her riding the river that far, finding enough berries and eggs to eat, pulling fish out of the river, staying out of sight of the Dakotas and Arikaras. Think of the heart it must have taken just to imagine the trip—and then to plan it and actually strike out on her own.

I didn't have that far to go, I told myself. Maybe six days on the river, if I could ever get to it. I stopped to pant and to smear my filthy arm across my filthy forehead. My hands, even as used to swinging a hoe as they were, had swollen from dragging the travois. This was a job for a horse. A small fear slowly climbed the back of my neck. *You're alone,* it whispered. *Everything depends on you.* I breathed deeply, gathering hope from the progress I had already made. I looked forward, not behind.

Open space plays such tricks on the eye. It shows you a sharp, bright line between earth and sky, but the farther you follow it, the farther it moves away. This was just like the line I felt in me. Somewhere, my father was alive and pulling his red hair. Somewhere, my mothers were losing hope. My anger toward him pushed me toward them. If it weren't for white men like him, if it weren't for the fur trade and the steamboat, I would be safe at home, instead of scared to death out on the prairie. But maybe he wasn't alive. When I thought of him killed by Dakotas, I could hardly take another step.

White Crane and Goes to Next Timber were impossible to please; sometimes their ignorance was embarrassing, and it pushed me toward him. They had no interest in reading and writing; they could be so nervous and silly in front of the men at Fort Clark. Sometimes I hated them and wished I were born to white mothers in St. Louis. But then I hated myself even more for disappointing them and for making them worry.

The line in me between red and white was as fine as the line at the edge of the sky, yet I seemed to cross it back and forth a hundred times a day. You would think I could decide which way to be.

Behind me, my poles had left two white furrows through

the blackened prairie. Young Wolf, or even Tom Hatcher, could follow this track at a gallop. Ahead of me, the burn stopped in a ragged edge, and beyond it, buffalo grass grew new and green among the amber stalks of last year. Something about the wind here must have let the flames charge only to the brow of this low hill, and no farther. Due east, beyond the hill, the heavy green heads of cottonwood trees nodded over the flood plain. I couldn't see the river yet, but I knew it was there, muscling its way past the trees, rounding the bluffs. I tugged my travois forward.

The unburnt prairie. After miles of char and crust, the cushion of live grasses under my feet filled me with joy. I plucked handfuls of half-grown bluestem and buffalo grass and buried my nose in them. Even the breeze was fresher and more alive here. Crossing the brow of the hill, I could see why that was so. Directly to my left, a narrow slough swung in from the northwest, making its way casually toward the river. Rushes stood tall in the shallows, and along its banks, thick stands of willow and ash almost hid it from view. Buffalo birds, song sparrows, and robins called cheerily, tree to tree. Farther downstream, the slow water rounded a bend and disappeared from sight.

This is your real test, I told myself. Muskrat Woman would hardly blink right now. I desperately wanted to drop my load and run to the water, to dunk myself time and again under the cool surface. Instead, I breathed deep, nodded my thanks to Lone Man, wherever he was, and plodded forward into the trees. Later, there would be time to rest, but not just yet.

18 July 1837

A heavy rain and thunderstorm this morning, splatter-
ing the world with mud, then moving off northeast.
Strangely silent otherwise. No news but smallpox. We
have heard it appears now among the Arikaras (the
"Rees," to Chardon), though the Minnetarees have so
far managed to avoid it. A canoe from Ft. Union reports
the steamboat blessed them, too, with the pestilence. "La
peste," as Chardon calls it. The story was the same.
Some wise soul tried to quarantine the boat, but was
overruled by ignorant whites and Indians, both eager for
trade at any cost. It will cost them dear. La peste will
cost them dear.

Having been inoculated some years ago in
Philadelphia, I can move freely among the sick here,
offering what little service they will accept and taking
such notes as seem warranted for the sake of science. The
sores of the afflicted are most distressing and painful, as
they spread in angry lumps across the face and limbs. In
addition, some of the sick have strangely died within a
week after the first fever and belly pains. They expire, it
seems, of sorrow, without a sore upon them.

Four

~~~

I stood well hidden in the brush, considering. A bull boat isn't hard to make if you've done it a time or two. Unfortunately, I had only watched. My mothers had let me stand by and hand them rawhide lashings, but Goes to Next Timber wasn't a patient person, and White Crane didn't like mistakes. Later, they always said; next time they would let me work on it. Well, *this* was next time, and where were they to teach me?

I knew the idea, though. Make a hoop on the ground. Lash four long ribs flat across it and four more ribs going the other way. Then bend all the long ends straight up. Lash a second hoop to the tops of the bent ribs, to make a sort of cage. Flip it over, flop the buffalo hide over the cage, and lash the edge of the hide to the upper hoop. Then you smoke it over a small fire, and tomorrow you've got a furry, round-bottomed boat, as tight as a drum. I figured I could do all that—except for the fire part and the tomorrow part. It would be nothing my mothers would approve, but, then, they approved of nothing, anyway. If it floated, I'd be happy. If it went together quickly, I'd be more than happy.

It didn't go quickly. I picked out some wobbly willows to use for hoops and ribs. White Crane would have used stouter limbs, but she had an ax. My little blade did more tearing than cutting. When I needed more lashings, I had to peel the bark from the willows and dig up some ropy roots.

The lower hoop quickly appeared, and the ribs went across and rose up all the way round. It was working. I allowed myself a smile as I lashed the upper hoop in place and tipped the whole cage over. But when I dragged the heavy hide over them, the ribs all folded down to one side. I tightened all the lashings and tried again. Still no good. I jumped up and down and tightened them again. I beat it with a stick, I cried, and tried again. Four tries it took me just to get the hoopwork tight enough to hold the hide.

I laced the hide around the hoop rim quickly. When I ran out of lashings again, I broke narrow sticks to use like wooden pins or skewers. I tightened the final tie, then stood back, exhausted, to judge my work. Nothing was perfect, not one thing. The hide had folds and wrinkles where it should be taut and tight. Gaps opened around the rim, while twigs, bark, and various lashings stood out at all angles. My boat looked more like a porcupine than a drum. I allowed myself a tender sigh: yes, it was beautiful.

I needed to leave my shady little den in the trees before Young Wolf and Tom Hatcher wandered in on me. And there was no sense trying to cover my tracks; they'd see at once what I'd been up to. Carefully, I raised the boat to its side and began to roll it toward the river. The frame felt fragile in the heavy hide, wobbly, like it wanted to come apart in four directions at once. But somehow the frame and the hide liked each other. I pushed through the reeds at the edge of the slough and let it flop down with a splash. It swayed, it tipped and wobbled. It floated.

The slough was deep, but not wide, and it wound quietly through the brush and low hills, bearing me toward the Missouri in the most roundabout way. Maddeningly, the more frantic I felt—the more sure I was that Tom Hatcher was about to surprise me—the slower I seemed to travel. Clouds of gnats moved faster. A small beaver passed me by. Again and again, I had to pole my little boat into the channel, coaxing it along, impatiently pushing past drift logs and tree trash.

The cover of darkness slowly settled around me. I wanted to cry, to swear and hit something, but silence now was my only friend. More than once I imagined the sound of horses whickering in the reeds, or men's voices muttering. Just around the bend, I told myself, we'll see the big river. Just one more bend. After a whole day of racing the sun, it seemed that now I was trapped in a moss-clogged, water-logged moment.

In the end, before I could see the river, I could hear its wide whisper. The insect clouds grew lighter. I felt the air expand, and suddenly I was swept out of the slow-moving slough and into the current of the Missouri itself. I slumped down and lay trembling.

Above me, the moon was rising against the eastern sky. It must be rising over Mitutanka now, I thought sadly, and I hoped Muskrat Woman was looking at it, too. I even hoped my worthless father had got home safe. But thinking of him stirred my anger again. How could he drag me out there like that and let me be captured by that drunken fool Young Wolf? Drunken fool Injun, anyway. Selfish white, foolish Indian—between the two of them, I didn't have a chance. I took a breath and blew it out slowly. At least the river was on my side. Gradually, I relaxed and let the evening air and the motion of the water soothe me.

Cottonwood trees appeared above me now, and I admired their dark shapes against the sky. The first few stars scattered themselves among the leaves, looking for all the world as if they actually clung to the trunks and branches. Something troubled my empty head about this picture, but it wasn't the stars. Trunks and branches. Oh no. I scrambled to my knees, which set the boat rocking crazily. Immediately I had to duck as a huge cottonwood sweeper passed inches above my head.

Dead and dying trees leaned out at all angles, their branches sweeping the surface of the stream. Other trees were barely submerged, lying in wait to flip my boat and pull me under like they had done to Old Bedeaux. My heart jumped into my throat. While I was daydreaming, the bull boat had swung itself out of the main channel and was now sliding along the landward side of a long wooded island. I snatched my pole and steered outward, around the next snag, and then back toward the island shore. It would soon be too dark to steer at all, and I had no idea how long this island or this channel would be. I caught a leafy branch on the next sweeper and pulled the boat hand over hand toward the shore. I could sleep here on the island, and maybe in the morning I could portage across to the other shore. It would be good to let the buffalo hide dry out, anyway.

I scrambled out of the boat and hauled it up the bank. The soil was sandy, and moonlit grasses stood in clumps among the tall trees. I found a likely deadfall where the boat and I could lie concealed by limbs and brush in the dark. I let it down gently, bottom side up, and slid underneath. For the second night in a row, I collapsed under the shell of my buffalo friend.

19 July 1837

A party of Arikaras came today to smoke with the Mandans. Reported later that The Four Bears, great man of Mitutanka, is agitating for an attack on Ft. Clark and wanted the Arikaras to join him. The Rees will not countenance this, and the two parties fell out over it. Rees tell us they will side with us, their white friends, in case of an attack, and they will exterminate the Mandans one and all. For that, they may need to hurry. The smallpox carried away a dozen more today. Our friend Medicine Bird is down with fever.

Of interest is how differently the disease treats the races. I have read Washington's account, and he recovered in a little over two weeks. The epidemic in Boston killed one in four of the British. Here, the death rate is already nine in ten—worse even than I had expected.

Some die with extreme symptoms—faces disfigured beyond recognition, their pustules large and grown together into one great sore. Others there are who die quickly of thirst, their early rash having swollen shut the mouth and throat. Withal, there is a peculiar stink about them—an air no doubt that is unique to this disease.

Five

Dreams surrounded me almost before my eyes were closed. I dreamed myself looking over my shoulder, frantic with worry, as I dragged a travois. Willow branches swung at my head, mosquitoes whined in my ears. Flames charged over the hill, and wild-eyed buffalo ran away, their dark hides smoking. I dreamed of my little boat swinging around and around, branches reaching for it, tangling it, and white men's voices calling out to each other through the dark trees.

I saw Muskrat Woman, looking somber but kindly. *White Crane will be all right,* she said. *You have her fierce mind and your father's strong hands.* I looked at my hand, and it was white. I hated it. I turned it over and back, trying to rub the whiteness away, trying to cover it up with charcoal and mud. And then it wasn't my hand at all, but Red Bull's empty hand that I was holding. I looked again, and Red Bull's hand was growing bumps, and then the bumps were turning to white spots. His flesh went soft in my grip, and I dropped the hand quickly and washed myself in the river. Fiercely I scrubbed with sand, trying to make myself white again, while horses stamped and a man cried out in the night.

I stirred and slowly came awake, shaking the voices from my head. It was dark. Deep dark and too quiet. A heavy fog had settled over the island, so that I couldn't see the stars. Through the gaps around the rim of my boat, I could dimly make out dark shapes of tree trunks. That was all. Not a sound found its way through the fog. The insects were still. Even the river's wet murmur was muffled and far away. It seemed that I had stepped from my dreams into a dream world, silent, flat, and gray. For a long time I listened, not quite sure I was awake. Then the voice came again, like the cry of a hawk diving from the sky.

"Jacob! . . . Jaaayyycob!" A man's voice, stretched into a high, thin scream, then dropping to a sob. "Jaaayyycob!" It was the sound of a heart crushed by grief, the exact sound of the fear and loneliness that shivered in my own heart there in the dark.

"Jacob! . . . Mother, Jacob is gone! He wouldn't tell me where."

I almost jumped straight up. It was Tom Hatcher. I could see him now. He had opened his shirt and smeared himself with mud and ashes, and a large hunting knife dangled from one hand. He shook his head and spoke again, suddenly calm this time.

"Tom . . . poor Tom. Are you all alone again? Jacob isn't well, Tom. You must leave him alone now."

Madness. That's what my father had asked him: Does madness run in your family? I watched in shock as Hatcher staggered through the trees, his head thrown back, his mouth open and gasping.

"Jaaayyyycob!" he called. His voice fell away into sobs. "No, Tom! No! You must leave Jacob's arm alone. Jacob isn't well, Tom. Look at the sores on his arm. But, Mother— No, Tom, Mother will be angry. Jacob have I loved, saith the Lord! And Tom have I hated. Leave it alone, Tom . . ." He stumbled through a net of branches. My heart hammered against my ribs, and I clutched myself to keep from running.

Then on a sudden his mood changed. He began to whisper and laugh. He dodged behind a tree, slashing with his knife. He sang out in a light and rapid voice. "Tom knows what to do, Jacob, to get you a new arm!" He laughed happily. "Yes, yes. Tom's found one, hasn't he? Yes." He whirled, slashing and stabbing. "Get away! No! It's not for you. It's an arm for Jacob!" He crouched and turned slowly, the knife ready for battle. He laughed. "It's a knife for a knife, an arm for an arm! Tom couldn't find the girl, but he's found an old man, Jacob. Yes. So weak and helpless, just like the old Indians were. This old man will give his arm for Jacob. Tom will bring it back for the bad, sick arm he took from Jacob! Yes."

Tom Hatcher moved off, muttering, into the fog and dark. A deep silence closed in behind him, and then, one by one, the crickets raised their voices once again.

20 July 1837

One month and one day since the steamboat _St. Peter's_ hove into sight, and the wailing in the village is constant. Those who are dying call upon those who mourn. Those who mourn call upon their sacred bundles and their gods. All to no avail. All to no avail.

Six

The river pressed the buffalo hide against my back, and I tried to relax in its cool arms. My little boat bobbed and slowly swirled. I made no attempt to steer. I wanted only to disappear and get away from that nightmare island. As the sky grew lighter, the sound of the morning breeze mixed with the murmur of the water all around me. The cottonwoods stood sturdy on either shore, and some of them, leaning out, dangled green fingers in the stream. Beyond them, the prairie hills lay firm and perfect, as if Lone Man had rounded each one with his hand. I breathed deep and slow, feeling safe for the moment.

It was funny: the river was here, but the river was downstream at Mitutanka, too, and even down at St. Louis. Near here, the river was carving Like-a-Fishhook Bend; farther up, it was drinking the waters of the Yellowstone. I wanted to be swallowed by the river, too. As far as it reached, I wanted to touch it all, to be there all at once, just as it was. "I am the river," I whispered. And then, to stop thinking of myself at all, I just said, "River." River, river, river.

From somewhere, a faint sound came to my ears, almost like the faraway bark of a dog. It made me think of Little Raven. It came again, and I sat up to listen. Now the echoes rolled over the rounded hills behind me, and I knew what it was: gunfire.

A flash of motion on the western slope above the river. I could make out two figures running hard. One of them paused, something flashed, and he started to run again. A moment later, I heard the rifle shot. Far ahead of these two, a third figure rounded a stand of trees, changed direction, and dropped into a coulee out of sight.

It had to be Young Wolf and Tom Hatcher, that much was sure. But who were they chasing? In a way, I didn't care, as long as it wasn't me. Briefly I considered putting in to shore behind them, just to see if I could steal their horses, but the very idea made me shudder. I took up my steering pole, keeping an eye on the two distant figures. The best plan was to stay low and quiet, stay in the main channel, and let the river move me along at its own pace. I imagined myself as a floating log instead of a little brown boat perfectly visible on the water. That seemed to work— or at least the running men didn't notice me, they were so intent on their prey.

I steered toward a ragged pair of floating logs nearby. I didn't like to be so close to their spikes and broken branches, but at least they gave a little cover. I kept my eye out for a larger log, maybe one with twigs and leaves.

My last hunk of meat lay beside me in the bull boat. I

had tried to keep it in the shade, but it was starting to smell bad even to me, as hungry as I was. I waved a few flies off and went back to steering the boat.

That was when Frenchie Bedeaux came running from the trees on the near bank. Bedeaux! At first, I couldn't think. How could he be here? He had lost his shirt, and his scrawny chest was fish-belly white. Running, limping, hobbling desperately for the water, he waved both arms. Then it struck me: he was the one they were chasing. On the island, Tom Hatcher had said, "I've found an old man."

I didn't think. Back-paddling with my pole, I swung around to get closer to him. Bedeaux high-stepped into the river and struck out swimming. A raw burn ran up one arm, he had a cut on his chest, and both his wrists were bloody where they'd been tied. His eyes were wide with fright. Well, I thought, he's about as hard used as I am.

"*Merci, merci, merci,*" Bedeaux panted as I floated up beside him. "*Merci.*"

"No talking," I whispered fiercely. "You hold on and kick."

We reached the channel quickly with Bedeaux swimming and found a cottonwood drifting like a feathered raft down the middle of the stream. Tucking our boat among the twigs and branches, we put a long mile behind us before we spoke again. We were both much relieved. Bedeaux hauled himself up onto the tree with a satisfied smile.

"*Mon dieu,* girl, but you turn up at the strangest places."

"One could say the same of you. But at least I have my clothes."

He laughed. "That is perhap my most stupidest mistake of all my life. I know the moose who can outthink me." He smacked the side of his head with his palm. It was strange to hear Bedeaux making jokes. I thought it must be too much sun.

"How did they catch you?" I asked.

"How? More foolishness of me. I am on a long streak of it." Bedeaux glanced at the hunk of raw meat in the boat and raised both eyebrows. I passed it to him carefully between finger and thumb.

"You are the red angel of the river," he said around a mouthful. "*Merci.* I going to name this river after yourself, one day."

I wasn't sure I wanted to ask, but I asked anyway. "Do you know what happened to my father on the island?"

"*Oui, oui,*" he said quickly. "At least, I know the crazy man Hatcher believe that the father gets away. Who knows if he make it home." Bedeaux swallowed another bite. I let out my breath slowly as he went on. "Swaggerty is killed, four Dakotas are shot bad, but the Angus—he is gone on the little gray horse."

"How did you get away from the Dakotas?"

"Myself," Bedeaux said, "I take a bad step and fall in the river. Then I think, 'Oh, *très bien,* I swim away and escape.' But the rifle—how to swim with the rifle? Think, I tell myself. Thinka thinka think. Ah *oui,* I slide it down my neck of the shirt. Thees way, both arms are free to swim, yes? No. That heavy damn musket drag me straight to the bottom."

At this, I had to smile. Bedeaux said, "You laugh, yes, but I am drownding! I twist, I wrestle, but the rifle, it does not come out. Aha! I take out the knife to cut the shirt . . . and I cut myself in the chest! Oh, I am the biggest fool since sheep." He doubled over with glee. "At last, at last, I cut off the shirt. *Voilà,* I am free. But, also *voilà,* the rifle fall to the bottom. And *voilà,* I am naked to the sun." He sighed. "Ah, I don't know why I don't shoot myself instead."

"No rifle?" I offered. We both giggled.

While the Dakotas were beating the bushes, Bedeaux had slipped away in the water. He floated downriver and waited till mid-afternoon. When he walked back to the camp, he found it destroyed. The food was gone, the horses were taken, and both his canoe and bull boat had been slashed and sunk. In the morning he set off again, sometimes walking, sometimes swimming, till at nightfall he spotted the camp of Hatcher and Young Wolf on the wooded island.

"Very gentle fellows, they are. Here, please, have some fish. Have some cornball. Going to Knife River? Oh, we go there, too. More whiskey? In the morning, my hands and feet are tied."

I shivered, remembering Tom Hatcher's madness on the island. "Did he talk about cutting you?"

"Oh, *oui.* All day he talk about nothing else. He is completely the crazy man. He say the arm of old Red Bull not good enough. Must have a new one." Bedeaux sputtered on in French oaths as we floated. The panic I had felt the night before rose up in my throat again.

"Did he say anything about Jacob?"

"*Oui,* his brother. Dead of the smallpox, years ago. The sores so bad that the skin on his arm come off. All day, tied up, I have to hear this over and over."

"I think he killed him," I whispered.

"His own brother?"

I told Bedeaux about my night on the island. "If you cut off a sick boy's arm, that would kill him. Tom Hatcher needs to replace the arm he took from his brother."

"Oh, *mon dieu.* It is truly the death of us all." Bedeaux glanced over his shoulder and slid again into the water. In a moment, he was pushing us rapidly downstream.

21 July 1837

Heavy shower and several thunderbolts in the morning.
I spent the afternoon with the crew hauling hay.
Brought in four cartloads and put it up as winter
fodder. Several men came in today from the meat
camp, saying they have killed a fine quantity of
beasts. Welcome news, with 30 men to feed.

I have applied to Mr. Chardon for leave to spend the
winter in St. Louis. Among many other things, I must
have new spectacles ground. My eyes seem worse again
this month, and I begin to have the headaches.

Not a good sign—I came upon R.'s three-legged dog
today. If he's returned without her, there can be no hope.
I am surely not his favorite, but he slunk across the
yard as if to ask a question particularly of me. We stood
regarding each other for a long, sorry, and curious
moment.

Seven

W̲ake up, *m'sieur.* Wake up!" Old Bedeaux floated in the river, his arms wrapped around a short log and his ponytail trailing in the water. Somehow he had blacked out—whether from exhaustion or loss of blood, I didn't know. And I didn't care; I just needed him to stay alive and awake. I wasn't about to let him desert me like Angus had done.

I leaned out over the back of the bull boat, holding Bedeaux by the hair to keep him from drifting away. This is not the proper way to ride in a bull boat, because it makes the boat think you want to go for a swim. I didn't want to go for a swim. I wanted this worn-out old man to wake up so he could help me save his sorry hide. I shook his head by the hair.

"Wake up, you old sack! You snaggle-toothed, dog-faced, whiskery old lump." No luck. "Wake up, you worthless, greedy, mixed-up Frencher. Arrrrgh." I wrenched my neck around to see where we were going. A sandbar was coming up near the east bank. If I could land us there, maybe I could wrestle him into the boat and push off again. I gave Bedeaux a yank to one side and the boat began to turn toward the shore. He wasn't stiff enough to make a good rudder, but he'd have to do. As we drew near, the sandbar came up smoothly from the bottom to meet us. I dropped Bedeaux's head to jump out. First I grabbed the boat and settled it a short way up the wet slope, then I went back for the old man. He was sitting up in the shallows, flapping like a duck, and looking around for someone to blame.

"What you mean trying to drown me?" he demanded. "You little cow, you simpleminded squaw-girl. Can't you let a man sleep? You have to yank his hair out the head? You have to drop him to the bottom? What's the matter you?"

I didn't even pause. I picked up a stick and waded out toward him, swinging. Bedeaux just lay back and splashed water at me, laughing like an idiot.

With both of us aboard, the little boat sat low in the water, but it held up better than I expected. Aside from being rude and ungrateful, Old Bedeaux was handy to have along. He was a better fisherman than I, at least. Using a smelly strip of buffalo hide for bait, he rigged a hook and line from a twig and willow bark. Soon he pulled up a catfish, which we gobbled raw, almost before it stopped twitching.

Night found us safely in the main channel, making our way slowly and silently downstream through the dark.

"You think we've lost Tom Hatcher?" I asked.

Bedeaux puffed through his lips nervously. "One wonders," he said, glancing behind us into the darkness. "I think this man is a bad spirit. His mind is gone, and his stomach knows nothing but the revenge. Swallows every-thing in his way to find it."

"He blames my father. That's why he kidnapped me." I shivered in the night air. Bedeaux looked back again. His fingers traced the rough lip of a scab forming on his shoulder.

"Your papa can fight, I know, but he is mostly the man of the books. If this Hatcher is after him, there is nowhere to hide."

"Hmph," I said carelessly. "It's a little hard to worry about my father. If it wasn't for him, I wouldn't be running for my life right now."

Bedeaux spat in the river. "You know nothing. Your papa treat you like a son. You should be grateful."

"He dragged me out on a fool's errand," I shot back. "He let me be kidnapped, and then he disappeared. I'm supposed to be grateful for that?!"

"How you know he not looking for you right now? Trailing your trail."

"That man?" I snorted. "He couldn't track a horse if he was holding its tail. No, if he didn't get himself shot by the Dakotas, he followed the river back to Fort Clark. Right now, he's yelling at someone, or he's drinking whiskey with Mr. Chardon." Something caught in my throat as I said this. My eyes felt hot and I sat still, breathing through my mouth.

Old Bedeaux scoffed. "You are such the fool, girl. McCulloch, he drive the men mad with how he treat you.

Does a man need the powder and shot? Who must write his name? Rosalie must do it. Who will count the packs going on the steamboat? Garreau, perhap? *Mais non*, little Rosalie will do this. Who is to mark in the book for supply? Oh, Swaggerty? *Non, non*, Ma'mselle Rosalie." Bedeaux shook his head in disbelief. "McCulloch believe you are a son to take on the family business, instead of a half-breed girl for to work the field and make the babies." He put his fingers through a gap at the rim of the boat. "You can't even make the proper *bateau*—a girl your age."

This was too outrageously unfair, and I wasn't about to listen to it. I turned my back and thought of other things while the old man ranted in French.

"You have only one friend in the Fort Clark, *ma bête*, and that is your papa. You should pray to all the saints that he is safe and well. Because, if not, your days of strutting about the Fort Clark are over."

"I do *not* strut around the fort!"

"And in the village, so full of yourself. So ready to say how you make always the good trade, how you write the talking papers, how you can say the white languages."

"That is not true!"

"*Mais si*, it is true indeed. I am living here about nine hundred year, and never do I see a Mandan woman so full of yourself. You have only one friend in the village, *ma'mselle*— that old Muskrat Woman. But she not going protect you forever. If not for watching after you, she ready to die tomorrow." He looked away and shook his head in amusement.

"That old squaw, she is older than me. I should know, since I marry her one time."

In all his babble, this bit caught my attention. "You were never married to Muskrat Woman," I scoffed. I knew she had been married once before Spotted Hawk, but to Frenchie Bedeaux? Unbelievable.

"I surely was," he insisted. "It was some very much time back—before the smallpox long ago. And only for one winter." He looked into the dark and sighed again. It was almost touching; after all these years, he still missed her. I had to giggle.

"What happened?"

"Are you not listening?" he snapped. "I was being like you, girl. I was being the strut-about, the strikes-many, the famous French trapper. I was making the boast all the time, angry all the time, fighting, blaming everyone but me. Muskrat Woman, she don't like the coyote man. I come home one time and she has put my packs and guns outside the lodge. 'Enough,' she say."

Bedeaux shoved his big French nose in my face. "And she going say the same to you one time: Enough. You wait and see." He spat into the water. We floated quietly past a slide where three young otters were playing in the dark. We were silent for a moment, and then he chuckled.

"Spotted Hawk come around later and give me his horse. He say, 'I think the Minnetaree lodges are very warm in winter.' A good man, Spotted Hawk."

I didn't care about an old man's stories. No one had ever

spoken to me like this before. Only Young Wolf, the traitor, had been so rude and direct. *You think you're better than everyone.* So the Fort Clark men hate me, and in Mitutanka I have only one friend. *Half-white girl. Half-breed squaw.*

Was I not a whole person—only half? And which half? In spite of my wish to leave whiteness behind, I could feel my tainted blood dividing, coloring me half red and half white from top to bottom, like a terrible disease. I tried to shrink into one side or the other, but my very blood marked me as neither this nor that. And both sides hated me.

I curled up and slept while Old Bedeaux steered the bull boat through the night.

22 July 1837

Finally, Mr. Chardon is restricting passage into and out of the fort. In the village, prayers, wailing, rattles, and drums abound, but still none of the Mandans will take the most elementary steps toward quarantine of the sick. There is some talk, though without effect so far, of moving the healthy to a camp across the river. Threats of war are also constant. Minor attacks of red on white are frequent, though nothing serious to date.

Sad news. As it must, the smallpox has reached my wives' lodge. The two sisters have the sickness and are equally constant in both moaning and vomiting. I attend them when I can with fresh water, salts, and cooling rags to the forehead. The mothers grow listless, an early symptom. Others of the clan in other lodges are dying. Many are too sick to carry out their own dead. I have been persuaded to bury some of these myself. They blame the whites for the sickness, so they don't mind using me as undertaker. No platforms and no eulogies for these diseased dead, and no mourners but the flies.

May God forgive me, but I begin to find it all quite tiresome. My bright R. forever gone, I confess I have lost all fondness for these duller souls around me.

PART FOUR
Mitutanka

One

———⁓———

Frenchie Bedeaux and I sat in the floating bowl of soup that the boat had become—its ribs all broken and the buffalo hide soaked through. We were both wetter than fish. While I bailed water with cupped hands, he steered, looking for a good place to put ashore.

To me, this wasn't miserable—in fact, my spirits were lifting. I was sure now that we had left Tom Hatcher and Young Wolf far behind, and with every bend in the river, I could feel us drawing closer to Mitutanka. But with every bend in the river, Bedeaux had grown surlier and more worried. He argued about the smallest things, and he took every chance to make me feel childish and stupid.

Bedeaux picked a wooded shoreline where the cutbank had caved, making an easy climb from the water. He started up the mudslide while I sank the boat, whispering my thanks again to Buffalo and to Lone Man for looking after me.

"I wonder where we are," I said quietly as I joined Bedeaux in the trees.

"Southwest bank, five river mile up from the Little Village. About two mile on foot." He listened intently for a moment, cocking his head this way and that, and searched the shoreline for anything out of place. "There's a trail over that way," he said finally. "Maybe our pals don't think it's us if they see two sets of tracks together. They think you dead in the fire."

I snorted. "You're joking," I said. "A trail is a talking paper to Young Wolf."

"Well," he snapped, "then the trail, she is shorter for us, and the famous Young Wolf can just follow either way."

He sure was a touchy old man. I wasn't even trying to argue; I was just saying Young Wolf was a good tracker.

"If he's sober," added Bedeaux dryly. "Your fine brother-in-law can't put away the firewater long enough to take a deep breath."

"That's not my fault," I shot back. "I'm not a white trader. Who makes whiskey, and who brings it here? Not me; not the Dakotas."

Bedeaux turned away. "It is not for the child to lecture me—white child or half-breed."

I exploded. "Stop calling me that! I'm *not* white, and I'm *not* a half-breed. I'm a Mandan, you crusty, hunchbacked old mountain goat! If I had any white blood left, I coughed it up in the smoke, days ago." I spat on the ground. "And I'm not a child either. At least not *your* child. If it wasn't for me personally, you'd be stretched out on the ground right now, probably missing an arm and a leg."

Bedeaux folded his arms. "Little girl, we not have the time for this."

I crossed my arms, too. He wasn't the only one who could be stubborn. I had saved his life, but Bedeaux was taking me for granted, just like white men always did. Little girl, little Indian. Little ignorant savage. Well, no more. "It takes no time at all to say you're sorry," I declared.

"To say what?"

"To apologize."

His ragged eyebrows shot upward.

"Frenchie Bedeaux," I said calmly, "everyone knows you're very brave and very tricky, and you've managed to stay alive a very long time. But because you're only a white man, there are one or two things you don't understand."

"Is that so?" he said sarcastically. "And the Muskrat Woman's last grandchild is to tell me these one-two thing?"

"Quite so." Out of nowhere, my father's tone came into my voice. "Let's start with something simple, shall we? First of all, this is not the 'New World.' One doesn't stumble into a land with millions of people and say, '*Alors,* look what I've *discovered.*' Second, those who live here are not 'Indians' or 'redskins' or '*les sauvages.*' Trust me, my friend—they're *people,* same as you!" Suddenly I was about to burst with anger.

"Most important," I said through clenched teeth, "you wouldn't be standing right here, right now, if this little Mandan girl hadn't plucked your filthy, freckled, pale-pink hide out of the river. Is that clear enough for you? I don't care if you're so old that you fart dust, Frenchie Bedeaux, you owe me your life. And you can apologize right now for acting like you're better than me."

Bedeaux was shaking his head slowly. "I swear, mademoiselle, you are the spirit and image of your crazy Muskrat Woman. Always, I am bested by this family of women."

He sighed heavily, then turned and started up the trail.

23 July 1837

This day came near to being my last. I was in the lodge tending the sisters, who grow more disfigured and out of their minds every day. Goes to Next Timber, too, moaned and cried out from where she slept. It is clear that none of them will survive, and I couldn't help thinking it is for the best. I sat alone, brooding.

White Crane entered, paused, and decided to kill me. One moment she stands by the fire, complaining loudly of stomach pain. Next moment she's screaming curses—swings a burning log at my head. Singed my hair and nearly opened my skull for me.

Rosalie's crippled dog made for the door tout de suite, the coward. My head was ringing, but I managed to cuff the woman away. She snatched a bow and made to nock an arrow. At this, I returned the fire log to her rather briskly, breaking the arrow and, I believe, one of her fingers.

We wrestled over the remaining arrows—she came away with one and stabbed it through my sleeve. I made my retreat then, bleeding freely and fending off a hail of rocks, pottery, corncobs, and flung knives. Never have I seen the woman so savage.

Doctoring my arm later, Garreau quipped, "One can only believe this means divorce."

The dog followed me all the way to the fort—a thoughtful gesture, I must admit.

Two

It was as if things had come unstuck from the center. Scarecrows were toppled in the gardens, rats were foraging, and crows were rising and settling like flies. Sunflowers looked on with frightened faces.

From the direction of the village, I caught the faint sound of crying. I moved toward it and came upon a little girl. She sat on the ground, naked, with one filthy hand in her mouth and the other tugging at the dress of her young mother, who lay motionless beside her.

The woman looked up with eyes dulled by pain. She moved her lips silently, pleading for something, but at first I couldn't understand the words. Her cheekbones stood out, and beneath her hollow eyes her face was gray and pebbled with festering, white-capped sores. A pair of fat black flies tiptoed crazily among them. Only her knees stirred up and down, as if she was trying to run away. "Kill me," she whispered. "I'm begging you, sister." I turned away quickly to vomit in the path.

"Last Child, get away from her!" It was Muskrat Woman.

She took my wrist firmly. "Come. And you may not go to the village. There is more death there than you can imagine."

Suddenly I was bone-tired. All the fear and weariness of my nights on the prairie and the river, all the horror in the dying woman's face took hold of me. I threw myself against my grandmother and sobbed.

"I know," she whispered, leading me away. "But you may not do this now." She held me out at arm's length and looked at me very soberly. "Last Child, listen to me. The women in our clan are growing sick like that poor mother there. While you've been gone, the white man's disease has come again."

"Smallpox?" I whispered.

"Last Child, you're young, but you are not much of a child. You'll have to grow up quickly now."

"What do you mean?" It would take a dozen women to teach me the coming-of-age ceremony, the sacred-bundle rites, the dances and all. The very thought of it wore me out.

"The world is not going to wait for us, Last Child. Everyone is dying. It's getting very late for me, and you must take a woman's responsibility now."

"Please," I whined. "I'm too tired. Next year I'll learn the ceremonies. I still need you to take care of me."

"Stop this!" She was very stern, but her eyes were full of grief. "Last Child, that is not what I mean. There is no time for rites. We will save the sacred bundles if we can, but I think bundles and ceremonies are not protecting us now. We have to find another way to help you through this white man's plague." She looked away from me. "Your sisters already have the fever and the bumps. They may not see the full moon."

Had I been gone that long? My sisters might already look like this disfigured woman on the path? I began to weep.

"Last Child!" She shook me. "You must stop thinking only of yourself! Don't you see? There will soon be almost no one left alive."

"Then I want to die with the rest of them!" I shouted through my tears. After all I'd been through, she was being so unfair.

She took my wrist angrily and yanked me along. "You may die or you may not. But you will take yourself by the hair now and decide that you can face it, either way. There is no choice here."

"Grandmother, wait." Anything to stall her. "I need to see my mothers."

"Later. I will tell them you're with me."

"What about the child there?"

"That child is good as dead." Stoop-shouldered but ferocious, Muskrat Woman led me away from the walls of Mitutanka.

24 July 1837

The disease is definitely among the Dakotas now. A war party of healthy Rees and Mandans attacked two lodges of Dakotas down along the White River. Killed them all—men, women, and children. On their return, members of the war party took sick, having caught the pox from their victims.

Threats against Ft. Clark come nearly every day now. Young Mandan warriors stand outside the stockade and call absurdly for Mr. Chardon's life. Some would have taken it, but Ft. Clark men are loaded for bear. We travel outside our gates only in groups and armed to the teeth.

In the village now, two-thirds of the Indians are sick. Between the dying and the dead unburied, there is such a stench of sickness as I have never witnessed, sensible from a hundred yards away. I take a nip of whiskey now and then, to cut the smell of it. The dog looks disapprovingly from his corner by the door.

Three

~

"Grandmother, why can you go into the village but I can't?" Muskrat Woman lay on a makeshift bed of furs and branches under a lean-to we had built in the trees behind the village. She was resting while I tended the fire and stirred a pot of soup. Between us and the village, the dead ones lay quietly on their platforms. No one came out to pray in the mornings; no one traveled past us. We were well hidden from intruders, but it was lonely. Occasionally, sounds from the village drifted down the slope to us—sometimes gunshots or wailing. Sometimes the wind brought a bad smell from that direction.

"I think maybe I was wrong about Short-Eyes," she said. Muskrat Woman didn't approve of direct questions, so she wasn't going to reply directly. She was going to tell me something about my father that would eventually give me her reasons for keeping me away from my lodge and my family. I groaned. My father was not on my list of favorite people.

"I think maybe a lot of people were wrong about him," she said. "He went around telling us not to touch the sick people, not to use their blankets, not to share food. But that is so selfish and rude that people chased him away."

"He thinks the smallpox travels through blankets and other things," I said tersely.

"Yes. I think maybe he's right about that. This is a white man's disease. I've been thinking maybe it doesn't travel by spirits, like some of our diseases travel. Maybe it goes more like a white man, straight at you."

"Then why don't you get sick?" I demanded again. "You go into the village. You touch them."

Muskrat Woman lifted herself on her elbow and motioned me over. "Look at this," she said quietly. She hooked a finger into the neck of her dress and pulled it off her shoulder. Just below her collarbone was a scar, a small hollow crater about as wide as my thumb. "Here's why," she said. "I got that sickness before, in the first smallpox summer, but it couldn't kill me. This is all it could do that time, and now it leaves me alone."

"You're immune," I whispered in English. Even the word seemed magic.

"What?"

"It's what he calls it: immune. My father says if you live through smallpox once, you're protected forever. Your spirit is stronger than the disease from then on."

Muskrat Woman got up from the bed. "Yes, I can see

I've been wrong about some people." She began to gather some things—her pouch, her stick, a skin of water, and a small knife.

"I'm going now," she said. "When I come back, we'll make you a grown woman. You get your mind ready."

25 July 1837

War and rumors of war. No trade is possible now, nor desired. The only news is of attack and smallpox.

In the village, the drumming and singing and hopeless prayers continue. They throb in the night like a headache from the pestilence itself. Thought I would never say this, but how I begin to loathe these natives. With their noise and the pains behind my eyes, I must have more than one whiskey every night, just to help me sleep.

When there are gunshots, the dog disappears for an hour, but he always returns. I've come to think of him as a companion.

Yesterday an awful sight. A young man stood by his dying wife where she lay in the path between the fort and the village. Her limbs and face were ghastly—fully eaten up with the disease. "You were beautiful when I married you," he said in his grief. "Now you are ugly and you are going to leave me." And then he cried out, "I will go with you." Before anyone could lift a hand, he raised his flintlock and shot her dead. At once, he plunged a knife between his own ribs and died in agony across her body.

What will God bring us next?

Four

When a Mandan girl becomes a woman there are ceremonies. It seems like when a Mandan does anything there
are ceremonies. There are songs and dances to learn,
dresses to make, prayers to pray, gifts to give. Sometimes
there is fasting, sometimes feasting. Usually, there are other
people involved, but sometimes, if it's very urgent or a very
private matter, a person has to make up her own ritual.
Right now, I figured Muskrat Woman was making up
things as she went along. I trusted her, but if I was going to
become a woman, I wanted it done as properly as possible.

I walked down to the river and swam and scrubbed until
I was squeaky clean. I oiled my hair and combed it. I
scrubbed my deerskin dress with clean sand and brushed it
hard with needlegrass. The work cheered me. I began to
enjoy the idea of our little ceremony, though I still didn't
see the hurry. I gathered things to cook and things to burn.
I caught a fish and dug wild turnips. I picked sage and
sweetgrass, tobacco, and of course muskrat plant.

But when it came to painting my face, I was stuck. Had I been joining a proper age-society like my sisters had—say, the Enemy society or the White Buffalo society—I would have known what colors to use. But this was not a proper ceremony. I would have to make it up. I tried different combinations: black and white stripes, yellow stripes on red, black on red. I rejected all of those. I tried circles, dots, straight and crooked lines. Nothing seemed right.

This little game of Muskrat Woman's won't work, I thought, suddenly bitter. It can't work, and I know why: it's because I'm alone. Because I'm joining a society of one, which is nothing. Nothing, again. I slammed my fist against the ground. It doesn't matter what I do, I'll never be any more than one, alone—half this, half that; neither one nor the other, and left outside by both.

Somberly, I washed my face clean and sat waiting. I could hear Muskrat Woman coming down the path, her step slow in the evening quiet.

"I can't paint," I complained. "It's pointless. I'm alone. I don't even know who I am, let alone who I'm becoming."

"Paint or don't paint," she said flatly. "But look deeper. You know who you are."

That's not fair, I fumed. None of this will work. I'm not joining my friends in a real society—and if Young Wolf is right, I don't have any friends, anyway. I have no sponsor mother, there is no old man to pray over me, not even my worthless parents are here.

I took up the paints and drew an angry black stripe from my hairline down my nose to my chin. On one side of this line, I smeared myself red; on the other side, white.

"How's this?" I snapped. Muskrat Woman looked over and nodded without a word. "And you didn't bring my family," I went on, accusingly. "Not even a broken-down old warrior to smoke a pipe and bless me."

"I brought many things," she said. "Stand up." She looked me over, squinting a little, and brushed something from the front of my dress. "You look beautiful. Very grown up." Turning toward the trees, she curled her fist in front of her lips and made a quiet clucking sound. Into the firelight stepped Frenchie Bedeaux. "They don't come much older than this," said Muskrat Woman with a wink.

He took his cue from her, and together they worked as if they knew what they were doing. Grandmother murmured a song while Frenchie tied a heavy feather into my hair. He sang something in Hidatsa about the river and a buffalo, while Muskrat Woman lit the sage and the sweetgrass. When he finished the song, she stood in front of me.

"Last Child," she said, "you are young and often disagreeable, but you have your own kind of wisdom, which I've come to respect. You are also strong in heart and strong in your body. Most important, all your relatives need you to walk in the world as an adult for them now. That's why we're here tonight."

"Yes, Grandmother." I lowered my eyes, ashamed of the selfish way I had spoken before.

Frenchie waved the smoldering sweetgrass to the four directions as Muskrat Woman gently slipped off my dress. While he mumbled another song, she dusted me from top to toes with a feather fan. "We are taking off this old dress," she chanted, "just as you are taking off your childhood." She held out her hands and Frenchie laid a new dress across them. "This new dress is my gift to you," she continued. "You are putting it on as you are putting on your new stage in life."

The dress was beautiful. Made of sheepskin from the mountains, it was tanned a very light color and decorated with simple but elegant quillwork down the sleeves. A young woman's dress. Frenchie stepped forward with a long necklace strung with red and green trade beads and hollow white bird bones. "My gift to the young woman," he said gruffly as he hung it round my neck.

Muskrat Woman handed him a pipe and gestured for him to go on. Frenchie smoked to the four winds and began to pray aloud in French. I think he must have forgotten that I could speak the language.

"We call upon you, O *dieu*," he began. "Or Lone Man. Or whatever your name is. We call upon you.

"Myself, I'd prefer not to talk to you right now, because you've let an evil spirit onto the land and it is killing us all. For some of us, this is reason to think you've lost your wits again, and discussing a thing with you is not worth the breath it takes."

He paused briefly to glance over at Muskrat Woman,

who didn't understand a word of French. She gave him a somber nod. He then made some empty gestures in the air and began to chant again.

"So it's really this old woman and this half—this girl—who want to have a word with you. They have a little play going here, and they need a geezer to talk to God. I should have said no thanks, as I lost my religion some years back. But, well, the girl is tough as a boot—a thing I've always admired in a girl—and besides, she done me a good turn not long ago." He glanced aside again. "Plus, to tell the truth, I'm a little sweet on the old bag."

Muskrat Woman couldn't take her eyes off Frenchie as his voice rose and fell, and I had to bite my lip to keep from laughing. He moved to my right, humming and waving his pipe.

"Now, I shouldn't have to tell you, O Lord, but this girl is mixed. Her blood, I mean. The girl don't like it, but she's half and half. Muskrat Woman says she's special—maybe has the vinegar to live beyond this parlous time and make something new on the other side. And she thinks the tension in her blood may be what pulls her through.

"But she needs a fancy prayer to get her off on the good foot, because, ready or not, she has to be a grown woman *tout de suite.* Not old like the Muskrat Woman here—saints preserve us all from that—but a good bit older than she's ready to be. And since, Great Mystery, since it's your fault she has to grow up so pretty damn quick, some of us think you owe her a little protection. That's why we're here, and that's what we want. Protection for the girl." He stepped in front of me and gestured again in the air.

"So there it is. Do what you can. Name of the Father, Son, and Old-Woman-Who-Never-Dies, amen." Frenchie blew smoke to the four winds again and then he stepped back. "And if you want any more, you can sing it yourself. Hah."

Muskrat Woman put her fist to her mouth and made the clucking sound again. Silently, Medicine Bird came down the path. He walked slowly, breathing hard, and stood without looking at me. He was pale. In the firelight, his ribs and collarbones stood out sharply, and eight angry smallpox sores marked his face and chest. I sucked in a big breath.

"Now, Last Child," said Muskrat Woman, "this part of things is tougher. A young man has to be cut during his *okipa*. You have to do this." She nodded at Frenchie, who took hold of my arms gently from behind. From her pouch, Muskrat Woman retrieved a small knife.

"What are you going to do?" I asked, slightly worried now.

"Stand still, young woman. Each of us must suffer for our people from time to time." Frenchie's grip tightened, and Muskrat Woman pulled the neckline of my new dress down. With the blade, she stroked a quick half-moon into my skin. I yelped. She turned to Medicine Bird. With the same knife, she tore back a large scab on his chest. His skin twitched, but he made no other motion.

"Medicine Bird, he's like me," she explained. "Only a few spots, and he's starting to feel good again." She pushed the point of the knife behind his scab and dipped white mush out onto her palm, as she said, "Better from one who's beating the sickness than from one who's dying."

My last meal rose into my throat as Muskrat Woman smeared her hand across the cut on my chest.

26 July 1837

Rain in the morning. Surprising us all, Old Frenchie Bedeaux has reappeared. The man has more lives than a sailor's cat. I would like to hear the tale of how he escaped the island, but I have little heart to seek him out. It would only remind me that my Rosalie has perished while he lives on. I sought instead my dog and whiskey jug, two comforts I perhaps depend upon too often these days. But truly, what does it matter now?

The pain behind my eyes reminds me strangely of happier days. That boy courting the sisters—Wolf Boy—used to put on my spectacles sometimes and dance around the lodge. The lenses made his eyes look strange, too large, which we all found quite amusing. I'd give him whiskey, and he'd sing out something in his broken English—like "Drink me only with fine eyes, eyah." Then he'd rush at me, stopping inches away, his eyes bulging behind the white man's glass. Big joke.

He tried that once on old Muskrat Woman and she brained him with a summer squash. "Dumb Injun," she said in English. We all laughed until our sides hurt. Ah, the Mandans are such a joyful race. They'd all die dancing, if they could.

Five

～

*M*uskrat Woman had given me the smallpox—a little of it—hoping I could fight it off and become immune. My father called this inoculation. I expected agony, but I felt only her rough hand and the wetness of my own blood.

"Hold this on there," said Frenchie Bedeaux, handing me a white cloth.

"A handkerchief," I said, a little weakly. "What would you be doing with this?"

He just laughed. "Stole it off a dead white man. Let's eat, eh?"

Muskrat Woman gave him a bowl of turnips and fish. "And for supper, plenty meat," she said in English, and Frenchie sat down on a log to eat. I made up a bowl for her, for Medicine Bird, and then for myself. When we finished eating, she said, "You're a very brave girl, Last Child. That cut's going to make you sick, you know."

"I know," I said, carefully putting fear to one side. "But then I'll get better." I dabbed at the cut with the handkerchief. "It's right where yours is, isn't it?" Gently, I fingered my necklace and the tight rows of beadwork on my new dress.

"Oh, Grandmother," I blurted. "I don't have a gift for you. All my things are in the lodge. When I'm recovered, I'll go and make something for you."

"Don't worry about it."

I found the little flint knife near the fire. "Take this, then," I said. "It's all I have, but it's been very good to me."

"No, I think you need to keep that. It may need to go in a medicine bundle."

"But what can I give you?" Somehow, this had me rattled.

Muskrat Woman took my hands. "Young woman, listen," she said quietly. "The rotting-face disease has now taken your sisters in our lodge, and they lie dead on their sleeping robes. Goes to Next Timber is very sick in her belly and cannot move and cannot stop crying. The bumps show all along her face and arms." Muskrat Woman's words came down on me like a cloud of hot smoke. She squeezed my fingers. "White Crane Woman is very sick with headache and fever," she said. "She goes crazy sometimes and tries to hang herself or kill the Short-Eyes. Stabbed him pretty bad one time." I swallowed dryly, as Grandmother went on. "The men want to kill the whites in the fort, but they are too sick to do it. All the clans are sick. All of them, Last Child."

I tried to imagine all the clans sick at once, but it was too big an idea for me. Too horrifying. "In the Little Village, too," she said. "And the Minnetarees. Even the Dakotas are getting it. You've seen only the girl at the gate, Last Child, but in Mitutanka they are all so sick they cannot drag the dead from the lodges. Just as they were in my day long ago."

All my relatives. The face of the young mother at the gate rose in my mind, and I squeezed my eyes to shut it out. Two thousand people like that? I began to feel the smallpox rushing into my cut like a living thing, seeking out my life. Would anyone be left alive?

"My father?" I whispered.

Medicine Bird answered this. "Your father lives, but he stays in the fort all the time."

Frenchie added, "The fort men are in danger very much. They come out only in groups."

The hardest thing in not being a child anymore was trying to think of others first. What would become of me without family, clan, or even village? My fears crept around me like a pack of nightmares, and the fiercest one was the fear that I might die of my inoculation, alone, here in the trees and dark. But, as desperately as I wanted to be in the lodge right now with my mothers, even I knew they were in no position to protect me. In fact, they could die before I did—or go mad and try to kill me.

Nor could I visit my father, holed up with the frightened men in the fort. He would not be allowed to let me in, for fear of the sickness I was now carrying. Nor would it be safe for him to leave the fort and stay with me while I recovered. If I recovered.

Cut off as I was from both sides of my family, the bitter

feeling of division rose up again. I belonged to no one, red or white, and I loathed myself completely.

Muskrat Woman spoke quietly. "Now, Last Child, here is the gift you may give me." She dipped the handkerchief in water and began to wipe the paint from my cheeks.

"After such bad news," she said, "this will be difficult for you, but it is the only gift I will accept. From now on, you must not be divided in your heart—half red, half white. You must be a whole woman, Last Child—your own color. It is a very beautiful shade."

27 July 1837

Last night a powerful destructive storm of wind and rain woke me and the dog. He faced the door and growled for an hour, as if to protect me. A sad, comical sight. I drink to his health and loyalty.

Four cartloads of Ft. Clark hay were scattered by the storm, and the men hunting buffalo were nearly blown away. A minor whirlwind tossed down odd sections of the stockade. Then, today, the gunpowder shed caved in, the timbers being all rotten. It is as if the weather were toying with us. What symbol of civilization will be the next to topple here in the Great American Wilderness?

The smallpox. Oh, the smallpox. It is taking the nearby Rees and Minnetarees in numbers only slightly smaller than it is taking of the Mandans. From these, the Dakotas, Yanktonai, and the other Sioux have caught it. Word from the West is that la peste is reaching even the nomadic Crows.

This sad fort has become the festered center from which rivers of the plague have run.

Six

$\sim$

*W*hen the first signs appeared, I felt only aches in my back and head. I wasn't sure it was the sickness at all. Muskrat Woman stayed with me most of the time, to be sure I didn't sneak away to the village or fort. But I was quite content to dig turnips, gather berries, or make cornballs from what she found in the cache pits of abandoned lodges. We sewed a new dress to replace the one from my childhood, and to save my white sheepskin dress for special times.

From time to time, Muskrat Woman went out and came back with news. Always bad news. More sickness, more death. She felt certain this would be the end of the Mandan people. Things were even worse, she said, than the smallpox summer fifty-five years ago, when she was a young mother.

For my own part, I had decided to hope. This had worked for me on the prairie, and it would work again for me now. "Lone Man and Old-Woman-Who-Never-Dies brought back the corn and helped us rebuild from the earlier smallpox," I said to her. "Why would they abandon us this time?"

"I think the last smallpox came to us through the Crows, who brought it from the Comanches and the people far to the south and west. Lone Man is much stronger than the gods of the Crows and Comanches. But maybe he has never met the gods of the white men before."

I couldn't think this way; she was always a step ahead. To me, Lone Man was here from the beginning. No one was here except Grandmothers Mouse and Toad when Lone Man made the world. If he was unhappy, we must be doing something wrong. I didn't think the white god could possibly overpower Lone Man plus Old-Woman, First Worker, Mother Corn, and all the others protecting us. Maybe white men thought so, but that was their mistake.

"Anyway," Muskrat Woman said, "I'm a little angry at Lone Man. Things have gone too far. If he really is stronger than the white gods, then I'm angry that he ignores the prayers of his people. And if he isn't stronger, then I'm angry at his weakness, and I may start praying to the white gods to strike him down with the sickness. Either way, Lone Man's not here in Mitutanka. I've seen it. He hasn't."

My head ached from thinking about this, or from the sickness, or from her black mood. I wasn't sure which. "But you always told me hope is so important."

Her voice was dead. "There is nothing to hope for, Last Child. Nothing can stop this sickness. Maybe twenty of us will live, maybe fifty. We can't rebuild with that few—and some of them old like me. No," she said, "Lone Man is gone and his people are dead."

"I can't believe you're giving up, Grandmother," I scolded. "Why did you inoculate me? Why am I trying to live?"

She shrugged. "It's not the same as giving up. You may live. I hope so. But you can't save our lodge and you can't save our village, and you can't save our people."

"I have to try, though. I'm thinking this is why I was kept away on the prairie while the sickness spread. So you could find me and inoculate me and then I could recover and help the village to begin again."

"Well, you can try to stop the river with a leaf," she sighed. "I don't think the river will notice."

"You make my head hurt." Talking with her was so confusing.

"Last Child, you should listen better. I'm on my way soon to follow Spotted Hawk. I don't have time to tell you again and again."

"Tell me what?"

She put down her handwork and shook her head, chuckling, as she always did when I was too dense to understand. "Last Child," she said, "you cannot save what the holy ones have decided to destroy." She brushed away a fly and put her hands on her knees.

"I've told you this story before. When you were very small, I had a dream. I had a dream of children floating down the river in bull boats. They were frightened and crying, but the river didn't care. It was carrying them all away toward darkness. And then you were there—this light-skinned one, this angry one. You were leaning way over the side of your boat, paddling as hard as you could, fighting the river with your bare hands. And you made it; you turned your boat to the shore. I was so proud of you. But when I looked again, you were alone. You were the last child, standing on a lonely shore."

I had heard my naming story many times, but I had never understood it this way before.

"Now it is happening," she said matter-of-factly. "The sickness is sending us all down to darkness. You will be left to begin something new."

"But that's what I'm saying, Grandmother. We can build a new village—like you did before."

"Rosalie, no!" She had never used my English name before. My mouth was open, but I could not speak.

"You have to think larger," she scolded. "I know you feel two worlds inside you, with a sharp line between. You want to choose one or the other, but you can't." She made a narrow gap between her hands. "*This* is where you have to walk—in this line between worlds. Your relatives will need you there, and, trust me, it will become a far wider place than you see. Plant it, walk it, build in it, and know it as your own territory."

"I—"

"Rosalie," she whispered. "You. *You* are the something new."

28 July 1837

An attempt was made on my life this afternoon, and not by my wife. A young Mandan buck went skulking room to room with a pistol under his blanket, seeking me out. As it happens, I was resting in my bunk, having taken a medicinal whiskey for my eyes. He burst through the door, and if this crippled dog had not interfered, today would have been my very last. Between the two of us, we sent the redskin packing.

Day and night the Indians call upon their heathen gods. It is always a ceremony with them— crying aloud and gouging themselves with knives, as if more blood will appease the beast that stalks them. It is both pathetic and repugnant. It is no wonder Andrew Jackson and the others say the Indian is destined to vanish from the earth. Where oh where are the noble red men I used to admire? In all these years at Ft. Clark, never have they seemed so primitive to me. I confess they drive me to drink with their ignorant noise.

(My dog does not approve of strong drink. Will not look at me when I pull down the jug.)

Yet . . . yet the savages do know something. They know this pestilence is bound up with whiteness. That is truth and truth again. Because somewhere a line exists, and we have crossed it. Our entire work among these pitiable natives is now crashing down as surely as if we had destroyed it by our own white hand.

And now some further justice coming, since the sickness has reached into the very barracks of Ft. Clark. Two of the men could not leave their bunks this morning.

Seven

On the fifth day, my cut was inflamed and my stomach hurt fiercely. I felt hot all over. Muskrat Woman was dozing in the shade, and I lay down to rest, too, but could only toss and turn. I thought a short walk would help.

The path climbed through patches of green shade and sun, while in the distance the river sent up its gentle murmur. But as I drew near the village, the feeling struck me, even more than it had before, that things were not as they should be. Horses wandered like dogs through the gardens and trees, with no young boys to look after them. Through the palisade wall, I heard children crying in tired, hopeless tones, and sounds of pain or madness from adult voices. A powerfully rotten smell hung in the air.

I turned away from the palisade as a wisp of something cold slid past my cheek like spider silk. Another brushed my wrist, another and another—tiny ghostly breezes churning all around me. When I looked up, fourteen bodies lay in the sun between the village and the fort. Women, children, men, dead of smallpox and abandoned, seething with maggots at the gate of Mitutanka. I clamped my hand to my mouth and turned away, retching.

It was just as Muskrat Woman had described. The few who were not sick wouldn't dare to wrap the dead or bury them, for fear of catching the sickness. So these poor ghosts were left to wander, their sad bodies tended only by the flies and filling the air with a stench like none I'd ever smelled before.

Dread and fear knotted my stomach; tears burst from my eyes. The place was a dream of evil spirits. Where was my home, my orderly Mitutanka?

On the point of turning back, I recognized a voice from inside the palisade, loudly raised above the rest. It was Matoh-Topa, The Four Bears. What could this respected man be saying? I crept along the wall until I came to a chink through which I could see and hear him.

A throng of men—most of them sick, and some dying—filled the open plaza near Lone Man's cedar post. Weak from fever, the men fumbled with the pipe as it passed around the inner circle. Sores covered their faces, arms, and backs. And The Four Bears—how he held himself upright, I couldn't see. Even with the rash flaming across his body, he stood strong before the council, dressed for war, and he spoke fiercely of battle.

"My friends, listen to what I have to say. I am one who has loved the whites. I have lived with them since I was a boy. I, The Four Bears, never saw a white man hungry but I gave him something to eat, something to drink, and a buffalo robe to sleep on. Always I was ready to die for them. They cannot deny it. They cannot deny it. I have done everything that a red man could do for them.

"And look at me now: this is how they have repaid me."

Thick red sores swelled his broad face out of any human shape. On the great man's left side, the blisters had run together till they formed one long weeping mass from shoulder to knee. He looked as if he could bleed to death before my eyes.

"The Four Bears does not fear death. You know it. But to die like this—with my face rotten!—even the wolves will shrink from me in horror. They will say to themselves, 'Look, look at The Four Bears, friend of the whites!'

"Listen well to what I say, my friends, for it will be the last time you hear me. Think of your wives, think of your children, your brothers, sisters, friends—think of everyone you hold dear. Are they not all dead, or dying, with their faces rotten?! And this is caused by those dogs, the whites.

"Think of all this, my friends, then let us rise together and leave not one of them alive!"

Never could I have imagined such a scene—The Four Bears dying on his feet, speaking for a war against the whites. What he said was true: he'd been the whites' finest friend for as long as anyone could remember. Even Mr. Chardon called him the Great Man. The end of things has truly come, I thought. It's just as Muskrat Woman said.

My eye strayed across the listeners until it came to rest on a man sitting quietly toward the back of the council.

His hair was long and handsomely groomed, and, unlike those around him, his skin was smooth and bright except where the *okipa* scars stood out across his chest. He didn't show a single mark of smallpox. He carried a rifle and a knife, and at his belt hung a small drinking gourd. Young Wolf.

30 July 1837

We are in constant danger of being murdered when we go out. One man covered with rash came to avenge his brother's death by attacking a group of us—killed one and wounded another, before Garreau opened him up with a hunting knife. I fully expect Garreau to contract the disease now—a better revenge than the dead man could ever have hoped.

But this is what life has become—a constant horror of consequences. I can hardly wait the ten days for the steamboat to take me away.

Spoke with Bedeaux briefly this afternoon. Usually such a disagreeable man, but today, strangely, he showed a particular interest in the dog. We drank a toast to the loyal beast.

News from the village is that we whites have lost a fine friend. I raise another glass to the memory of The Four Bears, who died today.

Eight

*E*ven though I knew it was coming, it seemed the smallpox rose up like a snake in the path and struck me by surprise. All strength left me. My stomach cramped and churned; my pulse hammered in my head. Then the fever began, and soon I was shivering constantly, curled tightly under my sleeping robe. Muskrat Woman wanted me to drink—soup, willow tea, muskrat plant—but the sores had swollen my tongue and throat. Even in sleep, I could feel the rash stealing across my skin, swelling into little bumps. My joints ached. The palms of my hands and feet began to sting.

I tried to sleep, but dreams whirled me away to a strange place of pain and fear. I heard gunshots and the shouts of raiders. Tom Hatcher's muddy face, his wild unfocused eyes, rose up behind a rush of flames. I fled back to the waking world with a scream. My face burned with fever.

Around the edges of my vision, all was a blur, but in the center, the colors were brilliant. Above me, a magpie and her chick perched in the green branches of an ash tree against a clear blue sky. The chick was nearly full-grown, with large feet and shiny black-and-white wings.

If I turned my head, I could see Muskrat Woman by the fire sewing a pair of moccasins and looking out toward the river. Frenchie was there, too, and they talked quietly.

The young magpie hopped to his mother's side with his beak wide and hacked out sharp, demanding notes in a high voice. She moved away and he followed.

"The young are so cruel to an old face," said Muskrat Woman, glancing up at the birds. "They worry the lines into place with their questions." She tipped her head in my direction. "Then they search your wrinkles for one easy answer."

Frenchie nodded slowly, smiling.

The magpies jumped to a new branch, the chick still begging. Finally, his mother coughed up a buffaloberry and shoved it down his open beak. He was quiet for as long as it took to swallow.

"Not safe out here, you know," Frenchie said.

"Maybe you think it's safe in the village."

They were quiet awhile, then Frenchie tried again. "Her pa is nearly getting killed yesterday."

"He's a strong man."

"Maybe not so much anymore. He's drinking all the time—even the fort men are noticing." Muskrat Woman said nothing to that.

I had no patience for the young magpie. He could fly, he could open his mouth. Why didn't he pick his own berries?

If I were his mother, he'd get a foot in his tail feathers. "Shoo," I whispered weakly. "Shoo." Muskrat Woman glanced over, then turned back to Frenchie.

"I hope you didn't tell him she's here," she said.

"*Mais non*," Frenchie replied. "I am the fool, but I do what you say. I keeping the mouth shut."

"You should tell him to stop drinking. End up like Young Wolf if he doesn't."

I tried to sit up but fell back, my head spinning. "Young Wolf," I croaked. I needed to warn them. Muskrat Woman turned.

"I know," she said. "You just fight your fever, young woman. You've got enough to do."

"He don't see too very good anymore," Frenchie said, still thinking of my father. "Rubbing his spectacles till they nothing but scratches."

"What does he need with those things, anyway?" wondered Muskrat Woman. "Even when they're clean, they make the world a blur."

"His eyes—" I croaked, but the phrase ended in coughing. My throat was raw with rash. For some reason, I needed to explain how his eyes were not the same as hers.

"Is no use, anyway," Frenchie said, chuckling. "She don't understand. Too old and too hard a head."

I got my breath and tried again. "White eyes, white ways."

"What'd she say?" Frenchie asked. Muskrat Woman only smiled.

Nine

~

*I*n my fever:

I floated swirling in a small boat. The river passed me along as if I were part of it. River, I said to myself. River. But the boat was made too hastily, and soon it was soaked with water. My legs were growing wet and cold, but still I held on. Leaning far out, I paddled for one more bend in the river, and then one more.

Eyes watched me from the shore. Voices muttered— mad laughter and angry whispered taunts. White girl, they said. Half-breed. Injun squaw.

Slowly, my round boat became a dancing mask that floated above me, its face a smooth curve with round eyes. Magpie feathers stood out around the rim like rays of the sun, and two small feathers reached out of the mouth—a tongue for telling stories to the birds.

The mask drew closer, and it was divided down the middle—one side red and one side white. The feather tongue was whispering to me, whispering words that made me very calm.

2 August 1837

It is as if God himself has deserted us, and in his place
the Grim Reaper strides openly. A thousand Mandans
now have died. A thousand more are sick. Has ever a
plague struck down more lives in one small corner of the
world? Is it possible that this entire nation will vanish?

Myself, I have taken to drink—oh yes, I admit it
freely. Chardon counts dead rats. Which of us has lost
his mind? I ask you. But I have thought it all
through, these last weeks, and here is the straight of it,
drink or no drink.

The Four Bears called us whites responsible, and
there can be no doubt he was right. We came for the furs
and we will take them, all of them. Next, the land. Oh
yes, we tell these generous, gullible primitives that they
will soon be rich from trading with us. Rich. And we
give them another medal on a ribbon.

But in crossing the wide Missouri, we have crossed a
line we never knew was there. We have gone too far. And
now la peste. The natives extend the hand of friendship,
and we give them the white, white hand of smallpox.

I hold myself as guilty as any man, for I, too, have
crossed a line. I have taken an Indian to wife—and
not one only, but two of them. Any churchman could
have told me this was an abomination and sure to be
punished by God. But nay, I looked on outer darkness,
and I did not turn away.

Thus, now, my savage wives will die, as have all my innocent half-breed children.

And worse! Oh, I find, to my everlasting shame, that I loathe them deeply. As I loathe myself. I look on their disease, and I see the rotting face of both my sin and my punishment. They will die—don't I know it—in agony unspeakable, and I am the cause. I am the cause.

Ten

⸌⸍

*I*n my dream:

*Old Man Coyote was going along in a nice white suit,
and he saw some children taking out their eyes and throwing them into a cottonwood tree. The eyes would hang
there all glittering, seeing faraway things, until the children called, "Eyes coming back go plop!" Then their eyes
would return to their heads, plop.*

*"That's a very pretty trick, my Indian children," said
Old Man Coyote, wiping his spectacles. "Your grandfather in Washington will pay you very well if you teach
it to me." He begged and bullied until, finally, the children agreed to teach him. "But listen, Uncle," said the
children, "you can do this only four times—no more than
that."*

*"Don't you worry," Coyote said. "I would never overuse
a nice trick. Enough is enough." And he went traveling.*

*He came to a stand of cottonwoods near the river, and
Old Man Coyote threw his eyes up into the trees. Oh, he*

could see so well from there. "Eyes coming back go plop!" he called, and his eyes returned to his head. Coyote was very happy with his pretty white captain's suit and his pretty new trick he learned from the Indian children. He polished his spectacles and moved on.

When he had done this four times, Coyote thought about the children's warning. "Ah, four times? That rule was made for Indian country," he said. "But I'm from Scotland, England, France, and Spain. I'm from America, too. Surely it doesn't count for me." So he threw his eyes a fifth time into a tree, and for a fifth time he called, "Eyes coming back go plop!"

But this time his eyes didn't come back. Poor Old Man Coyote cried to his eyes again and again. He staggered around among the trees, weeping and crashing into things. Finally, he lay down in his clean white steamboat suit and he slept.

Some mice came by, and they began to clip his hair for their nest. Coyote woke up and caught one little mouse in his teeth. "Mouse," he said, "do you see my eyes up in the tree?"

"Yes, I see them, grandson. But they've got a rash and they're starting to draw flies. Do you want me to get them for you?"

Coyote didn't trust her.

"What will you trade to let me go?" asked Grand-mother Mouse.

"Give me one of your eyes."

So Mouse gave him one of her eyes. Now he could see from one side, but the little mouse eye rolled around in the socket, and Coyote had to tip his head so it wouldn't fall out.

Coyote stumbled away with his dirty spectacles on his nose, and he came across Buffalo. "What's the matter with you, Coyote?" Buffalo asked. "You've lost your eyes."

"Oh, Buffalo," Coyote cried, "a terrible thing has happened. I've gone too far this time." Buffalo offered his left eye to Coyote. He squeezed it into the socket, but some of it bulged out still, and the weight of it bent Coyote down to one side.

His neck twisted and his back bent, his spectacles scratched and his white suit filthy, Old Man Coyote went on his way.

4 August 1837

Couldn't drag myself from the bunk this morning. The day seemed black and hopeless as the night. Half the men in the fort are down with the pestilence, and half of those are raving mad. I could hear Garreau through the chinked wall calling out in his fever. The man is a bear. Sick as he is, he slams his hand against the wall and my whole room shudders. He's beset with fears and dreams. Keeps a pistol in his hand—to shoot Old Scratch himself when he comes to claim his soul.

My store of whiskey almost gone since I depleted it a good bit last night. And still no word of the steamboat.

From the look of my room, I have done some raving myself lately. In the darkness, I stumble over bones and broken things, fallen books, and logs spilled from the fireplace. Only my candle's flame knows which way is up. I surely don't.

The dog has been gone for two days now. Never thought I'd miss that crippled whelp, but I must admit he and my jug are better company than I've had in many a month.

Eleven

*W*hen I opened my eyes, my first thought was that my feet were sticking out of my sleeping robe. They were wet as well, but I was too weak to sit up and look at them.

My eyes wandered to the lip of the lean-to above me and beyond it to the ash trees, bright leafhopper-green against the blue sky and softly lit by the afternoon sun. Their leaves trembled gently, and I thought there had never been anything so beautiful. *If I could throw my eyes to the top of the trees,* I thought, *what a world I could see.*

The breeze was cool on the soles of my damp feet. My hair and forehead were wet, too; my whole body felt soaked from sweating out the fever. Slowly, I began to take inventory. Weakness. That was the main thing. I felt as if I'd been rolled, wrung, and pressed out like a wet hide. I raised my hands to my face and explored gently. My skin was cool, something I hadn't felt in days. And the bumps were down, much smaller than before. Only six had blistered and formed small scabs on my cheeks. I felt for the one on my chest, and it was a hard little shell, a crust about as wide as the end of my finger.

I had no headache. My back and stomach pains were gone. Aside from the draining frailty throughout my body, I had never felt better, never felt such release.

But something was wrong with my feet—that seemed clear. They weren't just wet; it felt like they were being rubbed with a wet cloth. Not rubbed, no. I levered myself into sitting and a black, furry, deformed paw came down across my wrist. Little Raven.

"You came back," I whispered. I felt so silly as tears escaped my eyes. He ignored me while his sticky tongue moved methodically between my first two fingers, then the next, then the next. His breath smelled of fish heads.

Muskrat Woman was humming quietly, and the sweet scent of wood smoke drifted to me from the fire. It was then I knew I was going to live. I sighed and fell asleep watching the beautiful leaves.

6 August 1837

Left my room only once—the day too clear, the sky too
bright for my failing eyes. Stumbled out under my hat
to inspect the rebuilding of the gunpowder house, where
the men all regarded me strangely. Sidelong glances and
whispered comments. Ignored my instructions—clearly
thought me mad. Let them ruin it. It will collapse in
winter, but I will be long gone.

Stopped in to see how Garreau's illness was progress-
ing. The stench of smallpox hangs like a shroud in that
room and is complicated by the heathen herbs that his
Arikara woman throws on the fire. At least Garreau is
raving less, and he seems to be sleeping through the
fever. His face and arms are putrid with sores, but I
begin to think he may recover—perhaps some hidden
strength in half-breed blood.

His woman sits near the door, sewing. Another
survivor, she was one of those who brought us la peste on
the steamboat. She's rounded the corners of the room
with hangings, nothing properly squared along the
walls. If it were safe, they'd be outside the fort, in
Garreau's round earth lodge.

I swapped her a piece of calico for what was left in
Garreau's jug. A question: is a jug of hootch half empty
or half full? Half empty, but it will do.

Returned to my own filthy nest to find a page had
been torn from my ledger book and tacked to the door.

Should have been angry, but truly I cared little. The note itself was illiterate.

L VIT.

Signed "B."

Have no idea what it means.

Twelve

*D*rink." Muskrat Woman tipped a horn spoon between my lips and I swallowed. Broth, from a stew of buffalo, corn, squash, and muskrat plant. I was getting tired of this.

"Enough," I said. "I can get up and make something else to eat."

"Some people can be so ungrateful. This is what got you through the sickness. It will make you strong now."

"It's about to make me sick again. One more taste and I'll heave all over myself."

Medicine Bird chuckled. He stood near the fire, a bowl of stew in his hand. "Your appetite will come back in a couple days."

Muskrat Woman turned away and got up, muttering like a prairie hen. She poured the broth back in the stew pot by the fire, then put her hands on her back and stretched carefully. Something was different about her. I felt I'd been asleep for months, and now that I was awake, I could see how much she'd changed. Her hands trembled. Her steps were small and halting. Little movements left her breathing hard. I elbowed Little Raven aside and stood up.

"Grandmother, are you not well?" I asked. She didn't answer right away, but went on muttering to herself as she tucked something into a bundle on the ground. I waited.

"Bodies don't last forever," she said, finally, not looking at me. "I think this one's about used up."

I put my arms around her. "Oh," I said, "you always talk this way. You're in such a hurry to join Spotted Hawk. But look at me—I'm feeling almost well again. You took care of me, and I can take care of you now. Besides, I need you; you're all the family I have."

"Don't be a child about this," she said. She nodded to the bundle. "Pick that up. And hand me my stick." She was acting more than strange, and I could clearly see that she felt ill. A small worry began to whisper in the back of my mind.

"Where are we going?"

"Not so far as you think."

Medicine Bird, carrying his rifle, went ahead of us up a sloping path toward the back side of the village. We moved slowly, speaking very little and stopping often to catch our breath. Little Raven hopped along behind. He hadn't left my side since he woke me licking my feet, days before. We paused in a leafy shade, and he sat waiting, testing the air constantly with his nose and lips.

"He does that because the air is so heavy," said Muskrat Woman. "Heavy with death."

"How did you find him, anyway?" I asked her.

"Bedeaux saw him at the fort."

"I'm surprised Frenchie could catch him," I said.

"No," Medicine Bird replied. "He led him here. The dog likes prairie chicken." I laughed.

Muskrat Woman shrugged. "Bedeaux is an old loon," she said. "He thought the dog had powers. Then he sees it with your white man in the fort."

"In the fort?"

"Old Short-Eyes is drinking too much, they say," commented Medicine Bird. "The dog was looking after him."

The air was still where we sat, and the light through the leaves colored the world in soft shades of yellow, blue, and green. "But why doesn't he come and find me?" I wondered aloud. "I'm sure Frenchie would have told him."

"Forget about it," Muskrat Woman said. "He's not the worst of them, but he's a white, still."

"You can't mean that," I protested. "I should forget my father because he's white?"

"You can forget most fathers either way. But The Four Bears is dead," she replied flatly, as if that explained everything. The Four Bears, who loved the whites, was dead. I looked at Medicine Bird, but he said nothing.

"Grandmother, The Four Bears died calling for war on the whites. I heard him myself."

"He died of an evil white disease. Are you not awake? All of Mitutanka is dying of an evil white disease. There is no love for whites here."

"My mothers love Angus," I insisted.

"Your mothers were thoughtless girls in love with copper pans and trade cloth. And now they are dying of the sickness he brought."

"Angus didn't bring it." I blamed him for many things, but even I couldn't let her say this. "Angus tried to *kill* the man who brought it! You know that."

She looked away from me. "The Four Bears is dead," she repeated. "There is no love for whites in Mitutanka."

I appealed to Medicine Bird, searching his face like a white man would. "And what about me? Angus is my father. Is there no love for me in Mitutanka, either?"

"You're a Mitutanka girl," said Medicine Bird, avoiding my eye. "You're not white."

"Young Wolf says I am," I argued. "Young Wolf says I don't have a single friend in the village. And what about Frenchie Bedeaux? Do they hate him, too?"

Muskrat Woman spat. "Young Wolf gave himself up to the white man's whiskey. He's more white than you are—a drunk, just like your father. And Bedeaux hasn't been white for years."

"Grandmother, if whiskey can change your color, then . . ." I floundered.

"Enough!" Muskrat Woman stood up. "The Four Bears is dead. Bring my bundle."

8 August 1837

Word is the steamboat draws closer. I would pack my trunk, but there's nothing here I wish to take with me. I care for nothing—neither cloak nor blanket, hat nor book. All are tainted with the pestilence, or the memory of it.

That's not quite so—I'll carry my jug and gun.

The matter of the note still puzzles me. "L VIT." It makes no sense, yet it gnaws me through the night. And who is "B."? I know no one of that initial—or none who can write. I copy it idly with my finger in the soot on my table.

L VIT

L VIT

Would it be a number? In Roman script, it could be 57. But no, that should be LVII. Is it a word? Not in any language spoken here. Say a vowel is missing. Try the letter "A" and we get LAVIT. Close to "lave," to wash. Does someone think I should bathe? Try "E" and we get close to "lever" or "leaving." No help there. Perhaps it abbreviates a word? Or two words? Who could know?

L VIT. It is writ large, so I can see it through these scratched lenses, but its meaning is a mystery to me.

Thirteen

*I*n long shadows, we came to the place where Spotted Hawk lay. Muskrat Woman wouldn't speak to me because I'd argued with her again. She was certain by now that I was either white or feebleminded—who else would contradict her so often?

She had made a narrow bed beneath Spotted Hawk's platform. It was neatly swept and had a bighorn sheep's hide for a mat. Muskrat Woman sat down and nodded to the bundle.

"Open it?" I asked. She didn't reply, but began humming to herself as she lay back on the soft hide. Little Raven flopped down beside her while I unlaced the bundle and pulled out a beaded pouch, a pair of new moccasins, a medal on a ribbon, and a doeskin, tanned white. Muskrat Woman went on humming as she took each of them from me. Medicine Bird helped her draw up the doeskin as a cover. Then he touched me on the shoulder and moved off toward the village.

Now that it was happening, I knew there was no use resisting, no sense in complaining. Her mind was made up, and I was exhausted. What was left of my strength had retreated inward, where it had all it could do just healing my body. So I sat beside my grandmother with my knees drawn up and my fists in my eyes, listening quietly as she sang her death closer and closer.

I was too tired even to be afraid—or else the young-woman ceremony we invented had done its work already. My fears crept around me again in the twilight, but I gave them hardly a thought. In their place, Muskrat Woman's song flowed over me, making me very sad, but peaceful, too.

In her song, I knew the joy of my Mandan people as they danced for Lone Man long ago, as they raised their beautiful farms in the flood plains, bested the Dakotas at trading, and welcomed the strange, greedy travelers Lewis and Clark.

I knew her frantic grief when the smallpox came to the Mandans fifty-five summers ago. The fear and guilt as she watched her family die—just as I felt now witnessing the death of Mitutanka. But tomorrow was there, too, in the song, as it was for Muskrat Woman and the other women who built Mitutanka here by the river. I felt their strength and determination. Tomorrow was no far moun-tain, because her song, like the river, touched all times at once. Something inside welled up and filled me and stretched all my seams.

Little Raven sat up just before I heard the footsteps. He

whiffed his tail once or twice and lay back. Frenchie put his hand on my shoulder.

"You need to eat, girl," he said.

I shook my head.

"Yes, go. I got a deer hanging at the lean-to. And I heating the soup." He pulled me up. "You go eat now. Come back in the morning. I going sit up with this old woman tonight."

9 August 1837

Maybe it's two words, missing vowels.
AL VIT. B.
EL VIT
Wait a moment. That could work. It's French.
Signed B. for—Bedeaux?
Oh, good Lord, it's "elle vit"—"she lives"!

Fourteen

I wasn't about to stay in the lean-to alone. As soon as I'd eaten, I rolled my sleeping robe and carried it back to where Muskrat Woman lay. I handed Frenchie a bowl of soup and spread out my things beside my grandmother. She was sleeping now, but woke from time to time throughout the night and hummed faintly to herself. Frenchie sat hunched on her other side, quietly sharpening his knife. Little Raven curled his back against my knee and sighed. Overhead, the stars gradually brightened and formed their pictures. The seven girls who climbed to the sky escaping their brother the bear. The bright smear of stars where Old Man Coyote shook out his tail after backing into the sun. To the south, shooting stars began to appear. They increased as the sky grew darker—a frightening number streaked away from the dome of the sky. I shut my eyes against them, suddenly feeling cold as the faces of my sisters, my relatives, The Four Bears, and the woman at the gate moved across my vision.

When I woke, it was still dark, but the glow of false

dawn was spreading along the eastern sky. Frenchie was on one knee beside Muskrat Woman, his face grim and his hand gently supporting her head. I scrambled up.

"Grandmother?" I said.

Muskrat Woman's eyes were wide, staring past me to the fading stars. Her hand lifted weakly and I grabbed it, clutched it with both of mine.

"Grandmother!" I said again. "Wait!"

But she didn't hear me. For a moment her eyes grew bright, and then she let go a long breath through the circle of her mouth. "Oh . . ."

Frenchie carefully let her head down. All at once I couldn't stand another moment in this world. My heart clenched like a fist, and I threw myself across my tiny grandmother, sobbing. I turned again to search the sky and there, streaking toward the south, toward Old-Woman-Who-Never-Dies, a bright star left its fiery tail.

"*Oui,*" Frenchie whispered, watching the star fade. "There she go. I lose her twice, but Spotted Hawk, he has her once again. Spotted Hawk is a good man." He carefully drew up her doeskin cover and tucked it tight around her body. "We get her on a platform soon today. Hey, what you doing?"

I had plucked his hunting knife from his belt. With my left hand splayed across a log, I raised the heavy knife in my right. I was thinking probably the index finger should be the one to go.

But Frenchie caught my wrist. "*Non!* You fool woman." I bit his arm as he twisted the knife away from me. I kicked him, I beat on him with my fists. Little Raven circled us, barking and jumping. Frenchie was older than dirt, but he was still strong enough to spin me around and trap my arms to my sides. Little Raven caught Frenchie's arm in his teeth, and we all fell to the ground. The dog snarled and yanked on the buckskin sleeve as Frenchie held me hard against him. I wept and wept. "*Tais-toi,*" Frenchie whispered, rocking me. "*Tais-toi.*"

Fifteen

⸻

Listen," Frenchie said. "You sleep some more. I going to the fort now, be back pretty quick." He did a careful search for sharp objects and then looked at me again.

"You going to feel this way some little while," he said quietly, "but not forever." He jerked his head at Muskrat Woman. "She want you to be strong, live good, not hurt yourself." I nodded, wiping my face with my hand. "Okay, you sleep more." He stepped off into the dark.

As soon as he was gone, I stood and brushed myself off. I moved deliberately to the log again and took my little flint knife from where it was hidden in the pouch around my neck. I looked at my hand, and then at the blade. Too small. Too light. I would faint from loss of blood before I could hack a finger off with this. Well, maybe later, I told myself. With a sigh, I sat down. I took a handful of hair and began to saw it off above my fist with the tiny blade. Slowly I worked around to the back of my head and then started on the other side.

Little Raven's head popped up and he growled low in

his throat. It seemed too soon for Frenchie to be returning, so I crouched down beside a clump of sage and felt around for a rock.

Gradually, I began to make out the shape of a man on the other side of the platform, stepping quietly toward where Muskrat Woman lay. He was dressed only in moccasins and a loincloth, two feathers dangled from the back of his hair, and he carried a rifle. Little Raven growled again, and the man stopped. He squatted, slowly pulling a hunk of dried meat from a pouch. This he flipped toward the dog. Little Raven snuffled it and lay down again to chew.

In a moment, the dark shape of the man was bending over Muskrat Woman. Muttering something, he reached down to pull back her doeskin cover. I was there in an eye's blink, raising the heavy stone high as I ran. The man was just turning toward me as I launched it with all my strength. It was Young Wolf.

Before he hit the ground, I knew he wasn't going to get up. He let out one long, arching moan and was still. I rolled him over.

"Young Wolf, you fool!" I whispered, kneeling down beside him. "What did you expect, sneaking up on me like that?" I hammered on his chest. "What did you expect? Got what you deserved this time, didn't you?

"Young Wolf!" I whispered again. "Wake up!" His breath shuddered in and out, but he said nothing. Grasping two of his fingers, I twisted until they popped. His eyes flicked open. "Young Wolf!"

"Ai, Muddy Feathers," he groaned. His eyes wobbled madly as he tried to bring me into focus. "You've killed me now."

"Well, you had it coming." I thumped him in the chest. "What were you doing here?" Tears ran down my cheeks as I hit him again and again. "You had it coming. You had it coming!"

"Tom Hatcher," he whispered. "He knows where you are."

I froze.

"I came to warn you. Thought you'd leave with me, but . . ." Young Wolf moaned again and his eyes rolled back in their sockets.

"Tom Hatcher—he's here? Young Wolf!" I bent his fingers again. Nothing. "Young Wolf!"

"Oh, hell," said a voice behind me. "Now you've gone and killed my little Wolf Boy."

I scrambled up. Tom Hatcher's yellow hair stood out raggedly; his white suit was filthy and creased with mud. In his right hand was a short flintlock pistol, and with his left he had Old Bedeaux by the ponytail. He was jumpy and short of breath.

"That ain't kindly at all," he said. "I wanted to kill that Wolf Boy myself. Now what am I gonna do for an Injun?" He cast around in the gloom for another Indian, then looked back at me. "Well," he said, "I got you and the old man again. I guess I can find another Injun back at the fort."

He twisted Frenchie's hair and pulled him close. "Now,

you gonna lie down there with Wolf Boy and be a good old geezer, ain't you? Don't want me to have to hurt nobody before it's time." He gave Frenchie a whack with the pistol and sent him sprawling. Young Wolf groaned; he tried to sit up but fell back.

Tom Hatcher leaned over him. "I thought you was dead!" he snapped. "You don't move until I say so, Wolf Boy. And no more whiskey. Tired of your drinking all the time." He turned back to me.

"What have you done with your hair, girl?" he demanded. "Who told you to hack it off like a savage?" He backed me up against the legs of the platform and took my hair in his hand. "Look at this," he said. "What good is this going to be? Huh?" He gave it a yank and I yelped.

In two bounds Little Raven was airborne, and when he came down, he had Tom Hatcher's wrist in his teeth. I shoved the man as hard as I could. He pitched over to one side with Little Raven still attached, rolled, and came up firing his pistol. Little Raven yelped and spun round and round, biting madly at his hip. Hatcher plucked his big knife from his belt.

"Stand where you are, Tom Hatcher," said a man quietly. "Don't you even breathe."

I never thought I'd be so happy to hear my father's voice.

Sixteen

*T*om Hatcher hardly seemed to notice the pistol pointed at him.

"Don't be silly, old man," he said. "You can't see the side of a boat with them spectacles of yours." Doubt flashed across my father's face, and in that instant Hatcher snatched my wrist and swung me between himself and the gun. "Now shoot me, Grandpa," he said to Angus. His heart thumped against my back, and I could smell the sour sweat that soaked his suit. Then he laughed. "You simpleminded bookkeeper, put your fancy pistol on the ground. You got no idea who you're dealing with."

In the deep shadows to my right, the feathers that hung along Medicine Bird's rifle rippled gently as he raised it to his cheek. But neither my father's gun nor Medicine Bird's was any use while I was pinned against Tom Hatcher's chest.

"Very well," my father said. "Tables turned. Suppose we negotiate for the girl? What will ye take to let her go?"

Hatcher began to back away, pulling me with him by the hair. "I'll have your eyes before I let her go," he said.

The line between earth and sky was growing lighter,

and, strangely, I felt calm. If smallpox couldn't kill me, I thought, I have so little to fear in this world. I felt older.

"Hey," Tom Hatcher taunted. "How you like your redskins now, bookkeeper? They look a little puny, eh? Nothing like a good Old Testament plague to take the fire out of an Injun village."

"You knew?"

"Told you I wasn't no fool, McCulloch. I seen before how long the smallpox can live in a trade blanket." He twitched. "My own brother caught it from a blanket."

"You did this deliberately?" Angus said, aghast. "Lad, you've just killed two thousand people in these towns and plenty more beyond. It's unspeakable, what you've done!"

"My own brother, I said! This here just evens things up."

His brother. Of course. Leaning back, I spoke sharply in his ear. "Jacob isn't well, Tom! You leave him alone, now."

Tom Hatcher stood stock-still. "Mother," he whispered.

"You leave him alone." I scolded, "Jacob have I loved, not Tom."

A growl rose from his chest. "No!" he roared. "Jacob have I *hated*, Mother! Jacob have I hated!" His fist trembled in my hair.

Quick as thought, the little flint knife was in my hand. "You must leave him alone!" Down I slashed—twice across his knuckles. Hatcher's face went white, and like a child he stuffed his bloody fingers in his mouth.

Medicine Bird shouted, "Last Child, down!" and I hit the dirt.

The rifle spoke, the pistol answered, but Tom Hatcher barely stumbled. With one hand still in his mouth, he put his other to his head, where a bullet burn was running blood. The path to the river lay at his feet, but he stood motionless, staring at the dawn as if trying to remember a name from long ago.

A moment passed in silence. Then my father, moving slowly, slipped a loop around Tom Hatcher's wrists and tied it tight. Beyond them, Frenchie was helping Young Wolf to his feet. Angus turned Hatcher gently toward the fort, but Medicine Bird blocked the way.

"Medicine Bird," my father said, "good work. Let's get him to the fort, young man. We'll put him on the steamboat and turn him over to General Clark."

Medicine Bird didn't move. "This one comes with me," he said quietly, his flintlock cradled in his arm.

"Can't do that," Angus replied. "He's a white man, Medicine Bird. White men will see to him."

"He killed no white men."

"All the same, my friend. It wouldn't be right."

Medicine Bird shifted his rifle very slightly. "Don't call me friend," he murmured. "The Four Bears is dead." Their eyes locked briefly, and then Medicine Bird took Tom Hatcher's bloody collar and pulled him away. As the sun broke over the skyline, we watched them disappear around the wall and into Mitutanka.

Seventeen

Grief is the hardest work of all. We spent the morning building a platform on which to lay Muskrat Woman. For a long time I stood looking up at her, not thinking a thing. There was a stone in my chest.

Young Wolf was still dizzy, so we helped him down to the lean-to, where he could eat and rest for a few days. His face was bruised where I'd hit him, his eye swollen shut. I covered him with a buffalo robe and tucked his rifle beside him.

"Rosalie." Angus put his arm around my shoulders. "Child, ye daren't blame yourself. He'll be right as rain in a week."

On impulse, I knelt and reached under Young Wolf. I sliced through a short cord, and his drinking gourd came away in my hand. I flung it into the trees. Then I took the little flint knife and laid it flat on his broad chest. "Here," I said. "Let's trade."

He smiled, closed his eyes, and started to hum. "They say that the women are worse than the men . . ."

Angus gave me a squeeze. "Let's get some things from the fort. The steamboat will be here before sundown, and Chardon's told it not to stop at the landing. We'll have to canoe out to it."

After the long day, my head felt dense, and my legs were wooden. "Steamboat?" I said.

"Aye." Angus caught my arm as I stumbled. "Chardon's letting me go for the winter. We'll run down to Fort Pierre, maybe farther."

"No," I said. "The mothers. I'm immune now, and I need to look after them."

Angus let out a long slow breath. "Rosie dear," he said, looking away. "This will be hard for you to hear. But I'm afraid you and I are all that's left of our little family."

I nodded, saying nothing. It was painful but not a surprise. The path became a dirty wet blur in my eyes, and my feet seemed to find every rock within miles. Around my shoulders, my father's strong arm was a comfort.

"We'll start again, dearie," he whispered, "when we get back in the spring."

Medicine Bird stood at the landing while the steamboat idled in the main channel of the river, its paddlewheels backing heavily against the current. A few dry clouds shone copper and blood-red in the sunset.

"It's a strange time to be going," he said, looking over my head to the river. "So few of us are left here, and the harvest isn't in. We'll have a tough winter."

"There's no one alive in my lodge," I told him. "My father needs me at Fort Pierre this winter."

Medicine Bird raised his eyebrows. "I thought White Crane Woman . . ." He glanced at my father. "Well," he said, "you would be welcome in my wife's lodge. Our child is gone."

"It's a generous offer," said Angus warmly, "but I don't know how I'd get on without her now—what with losing all the rest, you see."

"You heard something about White Crane?" I asked Medicine Bird.

"Rosalie," Angus put in. "Now's the time, girl. Steamboats don't stand and wait."

"I just thought . . ." said Medicine Bird. He shrugged, not knowing how to finish.

"It's best not to dwell on it," my father said softly. "She would want us to carry on."

Frenchie steered us out in a borrowed canoe—a sturdy boat without any water to bail.

"Did you get Little Raven to a safe place?" I asked him.

"*Oui,*" Frenchie said. "He like his old room in the fort. And he like the prairie-chicken feast—very good for bullet holes, he say."

I smiled. It would take more than one crazy white man to kill a medicine dog. Angus tossed a small trunk aboard the steamboat and boosted me after it. "Look us up in St. Louis," he said to Frenchie. "Think you can keep from getting killed till you get down there?"

Frenchie grinned. "Why so? You don't want to miss it?" They shook hands, and then Angus swung himself onto the deck.

"St. Louis?" I asked. "You said Fort Pierre."

"Not to worry," Angus said, patting my hand. "Why not a visit downstream?"

We looked back at the shore, where Medicine Bird and a few of the Fort Clark men stood watching. Behind them, a sick woman draped in a blanket was stumbling down the path from the village. I turned to look for a place to lie down as the boat began to move.

"Last Child!" Medicine Bird called. He stood on the shore, supporting the sick woman with his arm. "Last Child! She's . . ."

My father stepped in front of me. "Rosalie, come sit beside me, lass," he said with a grand smile. "For so long I thought I'd lost you altogether that now I can hardly contain myself." There was whiskey on his breath. "Come and tell me all your adventures."

I pushed past him roughly and hung over the rail. "Medicine Bird!" I shouted. But he couldn't hear. He was struggling with the woman on the shore, who had dropped her blanket and was trying to push him away. She slapped him hard as he held her by one wrist.

The paddlewheels churned slowly.

"Rosalie," my father scolded, "come sit here beside me."

Now Medicine Bird tripped, and the woman staggered into the river. She fell, got up, and began to swim after the steamboat. Smallpox ran down both sides of her face, turning it terrible with swellings and sores, but I knew my mother's voice.

"Last Child!" she called out weakly. I got one leg over the rail before Angus caught me. He wrapped both arms around my waist and held me in midair as I screamed and kicked and sobbed.

"Let her go, Rosie!" he shouted. "She'll die before the week is out—and trust me, you don't want to see that." The boat lurched ahead. On the shore, Medicine Bird was running, diving into the water. He caught White Crane beneath the arms and towed her away while she flailed against him.

The two of them grew smaller and smaller as the steamboat bore me downstream.

Epilogue

July 19, 1845

My dear Daniel,

I admit I felt more than a little dread to find myself aboard a steamboat heading back up the Missouri. How ashamed I was to have survived when thousands died. Yet I took myself in hand, as Muskrat Woman would have wished. It is no accident that I, a survivor, now feel compelled to write the aftermath of survival. I intend to interview every Mandan still alive today, to take down their names and stories and demand that Superintendent Harvey in St. Louis deliver some just compensation.

The steamboat put me off at Like-a-Fishhook Bend, where the Mandans and Hidatsas—those few left alive of both nations—have established a new village together. Medicine Bird was as good as his promise. His wife's lodge is comfortable and warm, and she welcomed me as if I were not a deserter but a lost child come home again at last.

Medicine Bird gently confirmed that my mother gave herself up to the river as the steamboat pulled away, and he could not revive her. Young Wolf, like my father, drank himself into an early grave. We did not dwell on these things; what we face today and tomorrow is enough.

I am committed to my mission, Daniel, yet I fear my report will be horribly brief. Whole clans are gone. In two days, I've already searched out the names of every adult Mandan who survived 1837: 53 men, 67 women. Eighteen who were children during the epidemic also lived. My heart breaks at the sum. From a tribe of 2,000, fewer than 150 lived through that awful year.

"Plus one more than that," Medicine Bird assures me. "We thought you had disappeared, but here you are." Am I still Mandan enough to be counted? And how will the whites count me? How will they read my appeal for aid? This has become the shape of my territory between.

As I write this, Medicine Bird is playing with his

youngest child, a stout little girl with a wide, wet smile and two bright teeth. Grasping one of Medicine Bird's fingers in her fist, she takes two steps, bends her knees, and pops up with a piercing squeal. Medicine Bird, sober fellow, can't contain his joy. Alongside his tiny daughter, he steps and bends, rises and roars. His wife laughs, and even I must smile.

Neither they, nor I, nor the Indian nations have vanished. After years of fearful dreams, our laughter lights the morning air with hope.

Yours always,
Rosalie

Grandmother Mouse
and Grandmother Toad
talk to Lone Man

Lone Man creates the world
with First Worker

Mandans emerge from
underground

Old-Woman-Who-Never-Dies
sends the corn

Lone Man builds the wall

Coyote juggles his eyes

Mandans settle at
Heart River (1100)

First recorded
Mandan contact w
Europeans (1738

— — — *In the Time Before Time* — — — *1100* — — — — — *1700* ———— *1725* —

Time Line of Related Events

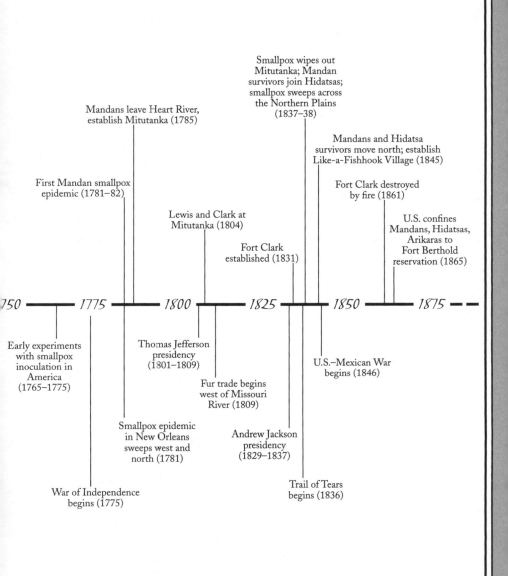

Smallpox wipes out
Mitutanka; Mandan
survivors join Hidatsas;
smallpox sweeps across
the Northern Plains
(1837–38)

Mandans leave Heart River,
establish Mitutanka (1785)

Mandans and Hidatsa
survivors move north; establish
Like-a-Fishhook Village (1845)

First Mandan smallpox
epidemic (1781–82)

Fort Clark destroyed
by fire (1861)

Lewis and Clark at
Mitutanka (1804)

U.S. confines
Mandans, Hidatsas,
Arikaras to
Fort Berthold
reservation (1865)

Fort Clark
established (1831)

750 — *1775* — *1800* — *1825* — *1850* — *1875* - -

Early experiments
with smallpox
inoculation in
America
(1765–1775)

Thomas Jefferson
presidency
(1801–1809)

U.S.–Mexican War
begins (1846)

Fur trade begins
west of Missouri
River (1809)

Smallpox epidemic
in New Orleans
sweeps west and
north (1781)

Andrew Jackson
presidency
(1829–1837)

War of Independence
begins (1775)

Trail of Tears
begins (1836)

Some Notes on American History

Last Child is a work of fiction, not a history book. However, Mitutanka was a real place, and the backdrop of the story—the smallpox epidemic in Mitutanka—is grounded in well-known historical events. The steamboat *St. Peter's* really did stop at Fort Clark on 19 June 1837, and smallpox really did step down the gangplank. In addition, though all the major characters in *Last Child* are fictional, some of the names and actions of minor characters are based on historical persons and what they did.

In the course of research, I studied historical documents of the period, later first-person accounts by Mandan and Hidatsa elders, plus works of scholarship from our own era. I studied traditional Mandan stories, Jacksonian-era politics, and medical facts on smallpox. I also paid attention to the writing of Native American scholars of today, especially where they discussed the unique identity challenges of biracial people. And I checked my treatment of Last Child's experience with relatives of mine who are biracial themselves. In other words, I tried to do my homework well, so I could plausibly portray what went on at Fort Clark and Mitutanka.

Still, I am neither Mandan, historian, nor sociologist. I may be mistaken about some things, and if I am, I apologize. I have included a list of some of my sources, and I'd encourage interested readers to study those sources for nonfictional accounts of life among the nineteenth-century Mandans and Hidatsas.

HISTORICAL FIGURES

Francis A. Chardon was the French-American "bourgeois" (managing officer) at Fort Clark during its most active period. Chardon kept a journal in English that is now a treasure to historians of the American fur trade. I depended on it for many details of daily life in the fort, and I used it as a model for Rosalie's father's journal.

Mr. Chardon was known, as were many traders, for his hard drinking, occasional rowdiness, and morbid sense of humor. He really did count the rats that were killed in traps around Fort Clark, as Angus claims. And in the early pages of his journal, he reports the grisly murder of two old people who had gone out to pick berries. This was the event that inspired the fate of Follows Crow and Red Bull.

Antoine Garreau was a valued member of Chardon's circle. Historians believe he was half French and half Arikara, and they know he served as Chardon's interpreter. In the novel, Angus mentions that Garreau killed a man and caught smallpox from the body, and this event, too, is one that Chardon records in his journal. Garreau recovered, for which Chardon was very grateful.

Matoh-Topa (The Four Bears) was one of the best-loved of Mandan historical figures, respected for his generosity, insight, and courage. His speech from the heart of the 1837 smallpox epidemic is one of the great recorded examples of Native American oratory. In *Last Child*, I have included most of the speech as it was found written on a back page of Chardon's journal. Some scholars are not sure it is authentic—how could Chardon have heard this firsthand and have lived to write it down? But others see no reason to doubt its substance, even if Chardon got it secondhand.

SMALLPOX EPIDEMIC OF 1837–38

From the sixteenth to the twentieth centuries, smallpox and other European diseases played a major role in the damage done to the First Nations of the Americas. When the epidemic of 1837–38 was over, more than twenty thousand Indians from the Upper Missouri nations had died. White observers called the region "one great graveyard." And this was only one epidemic. Smallpox swept across different parts of this continent many times.

There is a Native American belief, shared by some others, that white traders sometimes knowingly gave infected blankets to unsuspecting Indians. There is probably no way to prove this; however, we do know that some traders and agents prevented efforts to vaccinate the tribes they were supposed to serve. In addition, we know that Congress had set up a federal budget for vaccinating the tribes west of the Missouri River, and President Andrew Jackson spent much of it instead on his Indian Removal Policy—the policy behind what is now known as the Trail of Tears.

Vaccination and inoculation weren't common among Native Americans, but they weren't unknown, either. Chardon himself witnessed a Mandan father successfully inoculating his son, and this is where I got the idea for Last Child's inoculation.

It is believed that during the 1837–38 epidemic more than 90 percent of the Mandans in Mitutanka and Nuptadi (the Little Village) died. Years later, two men—Little Crow and Many Buffaloes Marching—collected the names of the survivors. It was a short list. Whole clans had died, and their secret ceremonies, histories, and sacred-bundle traditions were lost with them.

MANDAN CULTURE, STORIES, AND LORE

The Mandans were a matriarchal culture: the women built and owned the earth lodges and the farms. Men handled most of the hunting and the protection of the village. Mandan men often married more than one wife—often the wives were sisters—and the family lived in the wives' lodge. Grandparents handled a large part of teaching the children, while clans and age-group societies passed on wisdom and lore from generation to generation. Their location, their success with agriculture, and their sharp trading skills made the Mandans a powerful economic force in the northern Great Plains for centuries.

In *Last Child*, the Dakotas hover like a dangerous presence in the background. I apologize to any Dakota readers who feel this is stereotyping. Mandans certainly raided the Dakotas, too, but evidence from history seems to argue that the Dakotas usually outnumbered and outgunned them.

Stories were and are deeply important in Native American cultures. Some stories are sacred and should not be told by anyone without the proper rights at the proper time in the proper ceremony. Others are more general, educational, or just entertaining. The leaders of the Mandan nation have allowed some of these nonsacred stories to be published over the years, and I was glad to find copies of them. Parts of some appear in *Last Child*.

Still, one has to be careful with stories. Traditionally, one wouldn't tell many stories during the summer months—the season in which *Last Child* is set. You could think about them, of course, but, for example, if you tell Coyote stories in the summer, things might happen that you wouldn't like. Enough said. So the few stories I've included in the novel are nonsacred ones, they're already in print elsewhere, and they are not said aloud by any of the characters—they appear only as memories or dreams.

The story of Old Man Coyote tossing his eyes into a tree was told in different ways by several nations in the Upper Missouri River region. In her dream, Rosalie confuses some of these versions and mixes in details from her own life—as might happen in a bad dream. For a printed Mandan version of this story as told by Otter Sage in the 1970s, see Douglas Parks et al., eds., *Earth Lodge Tales from the Upper Missouri*. But my favorite version of this story was told by a Cheyenne man to a white folklorist in 1899; in his telling, he changed the name Coyote to "White Man." Think about it.

A very general form of the story of Lone Man and the flood is printed in materials from the National Park Service, available at Mandan-Hidatsa historical sites in North Dakota.

I've included songs from the Scottish side of Rosalie's family as well. "The Devil and the Farmer" is an old ballad from the British Isles. Rosalie also sings a few lines from "Widdicomb Faire," a scary old song with a very pleasant rhythm. The book of Sir Walter Scott's poetry that she mentions is kind of a family joke for me. In 1870, my great-grandfather bought a copy of this book, and it has been handed down from father to son since then. No one seems to want it. In 2002, my father gave it to me, and I can't wait till I'm an old man, so I can give it to my own son.

Selected Bibliography

These are some of the sources I consulted while writing *Last Child*. They address a wide range of issues, from smallpox to traditional stories, from life in an earth lodge to what it's like having both Native American and European parents. Many of these will be too advanced for young readers, but all will reward careful study when the time is right.

Beckwith, Martha W. 1938. *Mandan-Hidatsa Myths and Ceremonies.* New York: American Folk-Lore Society.

Bowers, Alfred W. 1950. *Mandan Social and Ceremonial Organization.* Reprint. Lincoln: University of Nebraska Press, 1992.

Chardon, Francis A. 1932. *Chardon's Journal at Fort Clark 1834–1839.* Ed. Annie Heloise Abel. Reprint. Lincoln: University of Nebraska Press, 1997.

Deloria, Vine, Jr. 1995. *Red Earth, White Lies.* New York: Scribner.

Fenn, Elizabeth. 2001. *Pox Americana: The Great Smallpox Epidemic of 1775–82.* New York: Hill and Wang.

Gilmore, Melvin R. 1919. *Uses of Plants by the Indians of the Missouri River Region.* Reprint. Lincoln: University of Nebraska Press, 1991.

Owens, Louis. 1998. *Mixedblood Messages: Literature, Film, Family, Place.* Norman: University of Oklahoma Press.

Parks, Douglas, et al., eds. 1978. *Earth Lodge Tales from the Upper*

Missouri: Traditional Stories of the Arikara, Hidatsa, and Mandan. Bismarck: North Dakota Indian Languages Program, Mary College.

Peters, Virginia Bergman. 1995. *Women of the Earth Lodges: Tribal Life on the Plains.* Reprint. Norman: University of Oklahoma Press, 2000.

Potter, Tracy. 2003. *Sheheke: Mandan Indian Diplomat.* Helena, Mont., and Washburn, N. Dak.: Farcountry Press and Fort Mandan Press.

Ronda, James P. 1984. *Lewis and Clark Among the Indians.* Lincoln: University of Nebraska Press.

Vizenor, Gerald. 2000. *The Everlasting Sky: Voices of the Anishinabe People.* St. Paul: Minnesota Historical Society Press.

Wilson, Gilbert. 1917. *Buffalo Bird Woman's Garden: Agriculture of the Hidatsa Indians.* Reprint. St. Paul: Minnesota Historical Society Press, 1987.

———. 1927. *Waheenee: An Indian Girl's Story Told by Herself to Gilbert Wilson.* Reprint. Lincoln: University of Nebraska Press, 1981.

Glossary

There are a few non-English phrases in the story that some of my younger English readers have asked about. These are not literal translations.

alors (ah-LOR): French expression for lots of things, like "oh my" and "well, well" and "just now."

bateau (bah-TOE): French for "small boat."

c'est vrai (say VRAY): French for "it's true."

Coyote: Old Man Coyote is an important figure in many Native American cultures. He is often called a trickster, but that's not all he is. In many stories, Coyote doesn't trick anyone at all but instead shows us the moral problems of selfishness, greed, and going too far.

de rien (deh REE-en): French expression for "you're welcome"; literally, "it's nothing."

Grandmother Mouse and Grandmother Toad: In one part of the creation story, Lone Man and First Worker were going along before they shaped the world, when everything was gray sand. And they came upon a mouse. "Hello, friend," they said. "Oh, you are not my friends," said the mouse. "You are my grandsons." They kept walking, and they met a toad. "Hello, friend," they said. "You are not my friends," said the toad. "You are my grandsons, and the ground you walk upon is my back." There is much to learn from this story, if we think about it.

Iktomi (ik-TOE-mee): From Dakota and other Siouan languages. Iktomi is an important figure in some Sioux stories. Like Old Man Coyote, often he's a good example not to follow.

la peste (lah pest): French expression for a serious disease or an epidemic (like the English word "pestilence").

les sauvages (lay so-VAZH): French for "the savages."

ma bête (ma bet): French for "my beast." Kind of a friendly insult.

mais (may): French for "but." Used often with "yes" and "no" to make it more emphatic.

mais si (may SEE): French. When someone says "did not," then *mais si* means "did too."

merci (mair-SEE): French for "thank you."

merde (maird): The French *s*-word. Save it for very special occasions.

moi-même (mwa-MEM): French for "myself."

moi non plus (mwa noan PLEW): French expression like "me neither."

mon dieu (moan d'yeu): French for "my God." Another one not to say in polite company.

non (noan): French "no."

Numak Maxana (nu-MAK ma-KHA-na): Mandan name for Lone Man, who is one of the holy figures in Mandan legends. He created half the world and saved the people from many disasters.

okipa (oh-KEE-pa): Mandan. This very special—and painful—ceremony is quite a bit like the Sioux sun dance. Sometimes a young man would seek wisdom through fasting and having his skin pierced. He did this to show the spirit world that he was willing to suffer for the benefit of his family or village. Often a vision would come to him during his *okipa*.

Old-Woman-Who-Never-Dies: A very holy person to the Mandan culture, she blesses the crops and is involved with certain animals and birds, especially the ducks, geese, and cranes that migrate over the plains of North America.

oui (wee): French "yes."

tais-toi (tay twah): French expression for "shush" or "be still." Sometimes affectionate.

tout de suite (toot sweet): French expression like "in a hurry" or "right away."

très bien (treh b'yen): French for "very good."

voilà (vwah-LAH): French for "see there" or "what I just said," but it is used for expressions as different as "there you go" and "ta-da!"

A Personal Note

In March of 2004, while I was in the middle of writing this book, Shawin-okwe, Lolita Spooner Taylor, passed away at the age of ninety-five. We were cousins, but she liked me better as a surrogate grandson—the odd one who lived too far away. Over the years, she and I shared many meals, studied our family history, visited graves, and wrote books together. She never got to read *Last Child*, but we discussed it often. Her spirit informs so many of the ideas in this book that I can't begin to tell the debt I owe her.

As a local historian, writer, teacher, and storyteller, Lolita was deeply loved in northwestern Wisconsin. Her Ojibwe name, Shawin-okwe, means South Wind Woman, and I'm sure there is no better image for her than that one. She took such gracious joy in telling about both sides of her unique American heritage that she made the "territory between" large and welcoming.

All her relatives miss her, not just yours truly. And for all of us, I wanted to close this book about the territory between in a way that she might have done. After telling a traditional story for children, she'd often clap her hands and say, as her grandfather did, "And for supper, plenty meat!" Then she'd laugh. "And if you want any more, you can sing it yourself."